Lauren's Library

property of Lauren E. Lason

W9-ABW-704

Praise for Firegirl

★ "Leaves a big impact." — *Publishers Weekly* (starred review)

★ "This is a thoughtful exploration of a brief interlude's lasting impact." — *The Bulletin* (starred review)

"In this poignant story, readers will recognize the insecurities of junior high and discover that even by doing small acts of kindness, people stand to gain more than they lose." — *Booklist*

"A touching story of friendship that is easy to read yet hard to forget." — *School Library Journal*

"Understated, beautifully written and deeply moving, *Firegirl* is a book that young readers will treasure for its ability to illuminate the elements of the human spirit that we all have in common." — *BookPage*

"Prolific fantasy author Abbott has created a realistic wallflower struggling to bloom." — *Kirkus*

"It's a beautiful story, a sad story, brilliantly written, a story you'll never forget." — Newbery Honor winner Patricia Reilly Giff

"[A] powerfully moving achievement." — *VOYA*

Firegirl

Tony Abbott

 LITTLE, BROWN AND COMPANY
New York ∽ Boston

Copyright © 2006 by Tony Abbott

All rights reserved. Except as permitted under the
U.S. Copyright Act of 1976, no part of this publication may
be reproduced, distributed, or transmitted in any form or
by any means, or stored in a database or retrieval system,
without the prior written permission of the publisher.

Little, Brown and Company

Hachette Book Group USA
1271 Avenue of the Americas, New York, NY 10020
Visit our Web site at www.lb-teens.com

First Edition: June 2006

The characters and events portrayed in this book are fictitious.
Any similarity to real persons, living or dead,
is coincidental and not intended by the author.

Library of Congress Cataloging-in-Publication Data
Abbott, Tony.
    Firegirl / Tony Abbott. — 1st ed.
        p. cm.
    Summary: A middle school boy's life is changed when Jessica,
a girl disfigured by burns, starts attending his Catholic school while
receiving treatment at a local hospital.
    ISBN 0-316-01171-1
    [1. Coming of age — Fiction. 2. Burns and scalds — Fiction.
3. Disfigured persons — Fiction.]   I. Title.
PZ7.A1587Fir 2006
[Fic] — dc 22   2005007964

                10 9 8 7 6 5 4 3

                        Q-FF

Printed in the United States of America

The text was set in Aldus, and the display type is Merss ITC.

For her

Firegirl

Chapter 1

It wasn't much, really, the whole Jessica Feeney thing. If
you look at it, nothing much happened. She was a girl
who came into my class after the beginning of the year
and was only there for a couple of weeks or so. Stuff did
get a little crazy for a while, but it didn't last long, and I
think it was mostly in my head anyway. Then she wasn't
there anymore.

That was pretty much it.

I had a bunch of things going on then, and she was
just one of them. There was the car and the class election
and Courtney and Jeff. But there was Jessica, too. If I
think about it now, I guess I would say that the Friday
before she came was probably the last normal day for a
while. As normal as things ever were with me and Jeff.

It was the last week of September. The weather had
been warm all the way from the start of school. St.
Catherine's has gray blazers, navy blue pants, white

shirts, and blue ties, and it was hot in our uniforms. I sweat most of those days, right through my shirt, making what some of the kids called stink spots under the arms. We weren't allowed to take off our blazers in school, even when it was hot, so mine always got stained from the sweat.

Like most afternoons, I got off the bus at Jeff Hicks's house. We jumped from the top of the bus stairs and hit the front yard running, our blazers flying in our hands.

"You ever smell blood?" he asked, half turning to me.

Jeff had been my friend for about three years, since the summer after third grade. As we went up the side steps to his house, I remember thinking that he asked me off-the-wall questions a lot.

"What?" I said.

Jeff always said some strange thing, then waited, and I would ask "what?" so he could say it again and make a thing about it. He reached the door first.

"Did you ever smell blood?" he repeated.

"What does that mean?" I asked.

"Sometimes my mom comes home from the hospital all bloody from the emergency room —"

We rushed through the side door, making a lot of noise in the empty kitchen. Jeff's house was always unlocked, even though it had been empty all day.

"— some guy's guts on her shirt," he said. "It's so

gross. It's the coolest thing. So, did you ever smell blood?" He yanked open the refrigerator door.

"I don't know. Maybe. When I cut my finger —"

"That's not enough. I mean a lot. A whole glass of the stuff."

I felt my stomach jump a little. "A *glass* of blood?" I said. "Who has *glasses* of blood?"

He pulled out a tumbler of red liquid — blood? — from the refrigerator and began drinking. He drank and laughed and drank. I finally realized it was cranberry juice. The juice sloshed all down his chin and onto the front of his white shirt.

His shirt had little blots of red spreading down the front as he was dripping juice and laughing and watching me, until I laughed, too, at the whole thing.

"Stupid," I breathed. "How long did you have that glass waiting in there?"

Laughing even harder, he put the dripping glass on the kitchen table and wiped his mouth on his cuff. "By the way, I went for a ride in it last night." He went to the basement door and pulled it open.

I was still looking at the glass on the table. "Huh?"

He jumped down the stairs to a room with a TV and paneling. There were dark wooden shelves on the walls piled with stacks of his comic books.

I was right behind him. "You went for a ride in what?"

It was that game again. But I already knew.

"Duh. In your brain," he said. "My uncle's Cobra. I thought it was all you ever thought about."

"Yeah? The Cobra?"

He snickered as he went to the shelves. "The Cobra."

A Cobra is a classic sports car from the 1960s. I love Cobras. Not the skinny kind they made for a couple of years, but the fat one. You see them every once in a while. A Cobra is low and all curved and super-fat, like a chunky bug that's pumped up like a balloon. It isn't a family car. It's just two seats, a steering wheel, and pedals on the floor. It's a machine. The racing tires are really fat. The wheel wells over each tire flare out like big, angry lips. The front end of a Cobra looks like a snake, with two headlights like eyes and a big mouth (the radiator hole) that could suck the pavement right up into it. It's the nastiest-looking fast car on the road.

I love Cobras. I've built plastic models of them. I've bought magazines about them. I once went to an auto show with my father, and they had a red racing Cobra there. The shine was so thick it seemed like if you dipped your finger into it, it would be hot and wet. But they wouldn't let you get near enough to touch it. "As if it's so hot it'll burn you," I remember telling my father. He laughed. Cruise nights at a drive-in restaurant in the next town sometimes had a Cobra, too.

That past spring, Jeff had told me his uncle had an

original Cobra, and I was totally floored. He had restored it from a used one he bought in New York, where he lives. I had never seen the car, but Jeff told me it was a red one.

"The kind you like," he had said.

People don't really talk to me much in school or notice me, not even adults. My mother says it's because I don't "get out there." But Jeff and I had been friends for a long time. We never really said much to each other, but we did stuff almost every day. I always got his jokes, and I think he liked that. I remember feeling it was so cool that he knew I liked red Cobras.

Jeff had said his uncle sometimes brought it up to his house, and he got to ride in it. But I didn't get why I had never seen the car.

"I've never even seen your uncle," I said.

Jeff was flipping through a stack of comics he had taken down from a shelf. He chose one and slumped in a chair with it. He didn't say anything.

"I don't have an uncle," I went on. "I don't get the whole uncle thing. It's just me and my parents. Neither of them had sisters or brothers." He still didn't say anything, so I just kept on babbling. "Uncles always seem like these guys who get to have all the cool stuff fathers never get to have."

Finally, he dropped his comic into his lap and looked at me. "Yeah, well, my Uncle Chuck has a Cobra. And he's coming over next weekend."

I think my heart thumped really loudly. "Saturday? Next Saturday?"

He shook his head. "No, the weekend after. The ninth I think my mother said. Maybe we'll drive over to your house in the car." He pushed the comic book off his lap.

"Really?"

He got up. "My mom said she got me two *Avengers* and a *Spawn,* the one where he bites through to another world. But she hid them because I yelled at her. Let's find them. I need to get all the school junk out of my head."

"Really? You mean it about the car? The Cobra? You'll come over and we can ride around in it?"

"Sure. Let's check her bedroom."

Chapter 2

Monday morning, I slid into my seat in Mrs. Tracy's classroom.

It seems strange now to think that I didn't know anything about Jessica Feeney then. She was only a few minutes away, and I had no clue that she even existed. I had spent most of Sunday sitting on my bed with my car magazines around me. The window let all the warm air in, and I remember wondering if it would still be warm thirteen days later when the Cobra came.

My seat in class was the first one in the first row by the hall door. It was odd that I was even in the first seat. Where you sat in all the classrooms at St. Catherine's was alphabetical. In every year before, there were kids sitting in front of me. Bender isn't usually the first name. Kids with last names like Anderson or Arnold or Baker were some of the ones who sat in front of me in fourth, fifth, and sixth grade.

Two years ago, a girl named Jennifer Aaron sat at the head of the first row. She probably always had that seat, I thought. But I also thought it was strange because I had heard that Aaron was a Jewish name from the Bible, and why would a Jewish girl be going to a Catholic school? When I told my mother about her, she said I should just go ask her. But I never did find out. Jennifer transferred to public middle school last year, and two girls from the other class, Tricia Anderson and Cindy Bemioli, were in front of me for sixth.

Jeff hadn't been on the bus that morning, but he was already sitting in his seat next to me at the head of row two.

He didn't say anything when I said "Hey." He just sat there quietly and chewed his fingernails, which he did a lot, without thinking. I guessed his mother had driven him in because he missed the bus. She probably wasn't happy about it and so they probably had a fight. Jeff seemed to get mad a lot more since his father went away. Usually, I just left him alone, and pretty soon he'd be okay.

Right now his head was bent to the side, and he was turning his fingertips in his teeth. His tie was loose around his neck, and his top shirt button was undone. I remember thinking that his mother must have washed his shirt over the weekend, or it was an extra one because there were no spots on it. Maybe they had a fight about the shirt, too.

His legs dangled out into the teacher's area at the front of the classroom. Mrs. Tracy had asked him a couple of times already that year to reel his legs back in under his desk. He was stretching them out when she came in just then.

"Scoot your legs in, Jeff. Your slouching will curve your spine," she said. "You'll be a stooped-over old man by the time you're thirty."

She walked past and set down a pile of papers on the middle of her desk.

"Thirty *is* an old man!" said Jeff, taking his fingers out of his teeth and half looking around and laughing.

I snickered when I saw him joking. Maybe he was okay again.

Mrs. Tracy narrowed her eyes at him then smiled. "You'll feel different when you're that age. . . ."

"I know," he said. "I'll feel old!"

"All right, all right," she said, but the class cracked up anyway. Another busload of kids came in after the second bell rang. Melissa Mayer, who was sort of chubby like me, came in laughing with Stephanie Pastor, who looked a little like a boy if you saw her from the right side. Kayla Brown plopped a paper on the teacher's desk then sat behind me. She was freckled and had red hair and was as small as the girls in fifth grade.

Rich Downing came running in and jumped into his seat behind Kayla as if he was trying to win a race. His jacket was under his arm, and his shirt was coming out in the back. When he tucked it in I saw the same little V-shaped rip at the top of the rear seam of his waist that I had seen for the last couple of weeks. I knew that Rich was trying not to eat as much so his pants wouldn't tear on him, but it was happening anyway. The pants I was wearing that year were ones I had gotten last spring and that weren't too tight, so I wasn't in trouble yet. Like Jeff, Rich liked to crack jokes in class, but he was never as quick or as funny as Jeff.

Samantha Embriano came by and sat in the last seat of my row. She had black hair and a round face and eyebrows that almost met over her nose. She always said her last name together with her first name: Samantha Embriano. Samantha Embriano. It was always like that.

It would be like me calling myself Tom Bender. Hi, I'm Tom Bender. Tom Bender here. You just don't do that. I think at first she said her name like that because there must have been a year or two when she shared the same first name with someone else in her class. Samantha Baker or Samantha Taylor. But she continued to say Samantha Embriano even though that was not true anymore. Now we all called her that. Samantha Embriano.

Just after first prayers, when everybody stood up and held hands together and prayed along with Mrs. Tracy —

"Hold hands? No way," Eric LoBianco said every time — I leaned over to Jeff.

"We're on for next weekend, right?" I asked. "Not this one, but the next one?"

"Next weekend?" he said.

"The Cobra," I whispered.

Jeff's face unclouded. He smiled. "Yeah. My uncle's coming over."

I smiled, too. Yeah, he's coming over and yeah, it's going to be awesome. Mrs. Tracy was still fiddling with something, and I scanned the room. I knew that no one else in the class was going to be riding in an awesome red Cobra next weekend. Or probably ever.

As I was thinking this and watching the last of the bus kids get into their seats, my eyes finally came to the last seat of the last row.

Chapter 3

Courtney Zisky sat in the last seat of the last row. She was the girl who I thought could easily be in clothes catalogs. Someone should pick her to be in them, posing with one hand on her waist, which was just the right size, and the other one flung up behind her as she pretended to walk. She'd be wearing all new clothes — a T-shirt never worn until five minutes before and flip-flops and shorts with flowers on them. Maybe there would be a breeze blowing through her hair as she tossed her head back but turned just a little to look at you.

Courtney was beautiful. She had dark, almost-black hair and her skin was sort of creamy white. She didn't have freckles or the pimples and blotches that Darlene Roberts had, who was three desks in front of her.

Darlene might even have been pretty good-looking if not for that, but in a different way. Plus, Darlene sometimes squeezed her pimples in the lavatory. You could tell, because when she came back, the skin around them was suddenly pink, like the spots on Jeff's shirt. You could also tell she was sad about her pimples and mad that she had them.

But Courtney was perfect. When I looked over, she was bending back up from putting something under her seat. A wave of hair went loose at that moment and fell from behind her ear across her cheek. It was like a splash of something. I almost looked away as if it were a private thing, but I didn't. The ceiling light flashed right off her hair and made it shine like a wall of dark water or something. The shine of her hair amazed me, but that was just one thing. I also knew that the smell of it was awesome.

One day, late last year, in Sister Robert Marie's sixth grade, I was able to move up a reading level because some of the books my mother kept pushing on me finally helped. My mom was so glad. And so was I, mostly because moving up that late in the year meant that no matter how badly I did, there wouldn't be enough time to drop me back down again. I'd begin seventh grade on a pretty good level.

I wasn't a good reader, at least not to begin with. All through first and second grade, and part of third, I was in the lowest group. My brain always used to switch letters around when I tried to read and the whole thing made no sense. And because St. Catherine's classes were small, everybody knew you were in the dumb group. Maybe

Courtney didn't ever call it that, but whenever people moved up, Sister Robert Marie tried to make them feel better by announcing that they were moving up.

"I hope you'll welcome Tom," she said that day. "Tom Bender is moving up —"

"From the dumb group," Jeff whispered loud enough for everyone to hear, because he stayed behind when I moved.

Anyway, last year, for a couple of weeks at least, I was at the same table as Courtney.

The first time, when she took the seat next to me, I caught a little scent of her in the air that moved when she sat down.

That was it. That's what really started it with her. That time she sat down. Gosh! It was like the smell of fruit or something. It must have been the shampoo she used. It was faint, but smelled like peaches and apples. Maybe that's what it was called. *Peaches and Apples.* Whatever it was, it filled up the space around her. Being so close to her was an unbelievable thing. If I ever sat behind her in class — which I never would at St. Catherine's — I don't know if I could ever get any work done. I would be leaning forward all the time and smelling her hair.

I nearly fell into a trance at the table that day.

But when Courtney began to read parts of the book she had chosen for the group, she spoke so clearly and with all the ups and downs in her voice that helped you understand what the characters were feeling, that I almost couldn't bear it when she stopped and Kayla began to read. Courtney seemed so excited at the exciting parts, too. It all just blew me away. She really was perfect. She was beautiful, of course. I knew that just by looking at her. But the moment she started to read, I knew she was really smart, too.

Since then, since that afternoon — on the bus, at night before bed — I had begun to think of ways I could save her life.

I couldn't be the only one who did that. I couldn't be. There wouldn't be all those adventure stories and comic books and movies and TV shows with all their action and lifesaving going on if I was the only one, would there?

Maybe it was from reading Jeff's comics in the afternoons or thinking about being in the Cobra or not being out there enough and having too much time alone, but I thought about saving Courtney's life nearly every day.

This is how it worked. It could be just an ordinary day — like today at school with the teachers and books and milk cartons and the smell of lockers and backpacks all around me — and I would suddenly sense that Courtney was in danger and I would have to rescue her.

For instance, Courtney and I would be the only ones at school, left behind because of something with the buses being gone and it was late or we were late. Then I would see her at her locker, reaching for the top shelf and looking up into the back of it.

Suddenly, the walls would begin to shake. The ceiling would rattle and the floor tiles would start popping up out of the floor. *Pop! Pop!* You could see them shooting up, silhouetted in the big square of light coming from the end of the hallway. I'd seen that light a million times before, only this time the tiles were popping right up into it.

Pop! Pop! Pop-op-op!

I knew right away what it was.

"Earthquake!" I yelled, running to her locker. Her hair was moving in a wave as she turned herself to the light then back to me. Ignoring the danger to myself, I pulled Courtney by the waist down the hallway toward the light. But as far as it actually was from our lockers to that doorway, it now seemed totally endless.

Pop! Pop-op-opppppppp!

We ran faster. Now the fluorescent ceiling lights began exploding one by one above us, the floor opened, and huge cracks appeared. A cloud of steam and flames burst up out of the ground under the school.

"I knew it — the center of the earth!" I said angrily. "It was just a matter of time!"

She looked at me, her eyes so wild. "But, Tom —"

I shook my head. "Just come with me!"

Dancing over the widening cracks, holding her closely, I drew her toward the doors to safety. We plunged through a small gap of daylight just as the walls thundered down behind us.

Standing next to her, breathing hard, as the police and fire engines and ambulances roared up around us, my arm still around her waist, I turned and smiled. "First period tomorrow's going to be a little tough."

She fainted then, but I caught her, moving my other arm swiftly up under her knees.

Chapter 4

But that wasn't all. I had lots of rescues.

Masked marauders — I always liked the word *marauders*, which I got from one of Jeff's comics, and of course they had to have masks on, really creepy masks with horns — would try to steal Courtney for some reason involving lots of money.

But there I was, battling my way past them, breaking the chains on her wrists, and carrying her up through some kind of tunnel of falling blades, which turned out to be not far from school when we surfaced. We dived right into my fat red Cobra and out of the parking lot, our pockets dripping with gold and jewels — enough for us to live on for the rest of our lives.

Or I would be at recess, flapping cool air into my blazer and talking with the guys about the science quiz, when I'd suddenly look up — I was the only one who knew to do this at just that moment — to see Courtney plummeting through the air. The jet her uncle was piloting was on fire and crashing.

"She bailed out!" I would say. "Stupid chute didn't open!"

Tossing my blazer aside, I would somehow leap up from the roof of the gym (I was on top of the gym now) and jump sort of sideways across the school yard and catch her just as she fell. We would tumble slowly and softly to the ground together, on the bright green grass of a golf course that was across the street, and her hair would fly across our faces as we rolled and rolled down a little green hill. Then it would get a little hazy, but suddenly everyone was crowding around us — Joey and Rich and Darlene and Mrs. Tracy and Samantha Embriano.

And there would come the moment in front of everyone when Courtney would thank me.

Thank you, thank you, thank you!

And she would always be with me after that.

It could happen.

A short snapping sound of loose papers being stacked on a desk made me lift my head. Mrs. Tracy called on Joey Sisman to hand back some graded papers. He started in the back corner, putting a couple on Courtney's desk. She nodded and then leaned forward, moving her right hand between her skirt and the desk seat.

She looked up, maybe at the clock, and I turned away.

Of course, Courtney Zisky never actually noticed me. She was popular and had her own big bunch of friends that had never included me. Why would it include me? I was just a sweaty, fat kid with baggy pants, and she was Courtney Zisky.

But being unknown was actually good. Here's where not "getting out there" was a good thing. Not being noticed was perfect for a superhero. And I sort of was a superhero in all the adventures I thought of with her in them. I was pretty fearless. I had powers.

I had powers, even though I have to say that there was a pretty strange thing about every rescue story I thought of. The powers I had were not the usual superhero ones. They were small. Little powers. Not very remarkable. You could say they were even dumb.

In my battle against the marauders, for instance, I didn't have amazing strength or superspeed. When it came to the big moment to rescue Courtney, I found that what I could do was spin really fast — so fast I was like a blur! — on one foot.

If spinning fast was almost worthless in most situations, it happened to be the perfect thing against the marauders. They could do nothing against my spinning around. They fell away from me, dropping their weapons, which clanked to the floor. Their mouths (I could see their mouths behind the masks) were open wide and yelling. Their eyes were full of fear. Finally, I stopped spinning long enough to pull Courtney away to freedom. We lived a happy life after that.

One-foot spinning was not all I could do, though.

Sometimes a hand made of glue was the one thing I needed to stop the bad men. Once I used a detachable ear to trick them. A very loud finger snap, invisible elbows, an earthshaking hum, legs of snow, and the ability to roll uphill were just some of the many powers that helped me in my Courtney stories.

Each time, before I hopped into my famous roaring red Cobra and tore off into the night with her, I would use one of these abilities and leave all the powerful evildoers falling down in defeat.

Not that these rescues were ever easy.

Some of them were very tough. A lot of the time there would be a point when I'd have to choose between two really horrible things to save Courtney.

It was either the pit of hissing snakes or the rushing bunch of sweaty men with big iron clubs. The stairway of flashing sabres or the man-eating–snake-infested pool that stank like garbage.

Faced with these kinds of dangers, there came a moment when everything stopped and an instant of complete stillness fell over me and over everything around me.

I stood there, sizing up my choices.

It was like I was standing in the middle of a flimsy, little rope bridge. On one side the ropes were on fire, burning away from the rocks that held them. On the other was a troop of sword-waving bandits with painted faces charging at me.

At this moment in the soundtrack — my adventures were always accompanied by booming horns and thundering drums — everything would go silent except for a single long note played on a violin, a note as thin and sharp as a thread (like the thread that held up that bridge I was on).

While that one note played, everything stopped. The bridge didn't burn. The bad guys didn't charge. No one breathed.

Sometimes, that violin note went on too long and my daydreams faded away. Someone would snap some papers or the school bell would ring or a bus would honk its horn, and the adventure couldn't go on. Then I would look around and pretend to be with everybody else again, which meant that I'd have to start at the beginning of the story. That was okay, too. The start of the adventure was the best part, anyway. I had lots of beginnings about how I could be the only one to really save Courtney.

There was a sharp knock at the classroom door. It opened a crack, and I heard a voice say "Linda?" Mrs. Tracy went into the hall for a second then came back with a pink note.

I looked again and Courtney was reading. I didn't

imagine that I was completely alone in feeling something for her. She was really too beautiful for me to be the only one. From the way Jeff acted when she was around, I half suspected that he liked her, too. Sometimes he seemed to worm his way close to her in the lunch line, nudging ahead of the others in a way that looked almost natural. I tried not to worry too much about it because Jeff never actually seemed to talk to Courtney. He never talked *about* her with me, that's for sure.

I had decided that the best thing was never to bring up the subject, even though Jeff was the only other kid I had ever talked to about very much at all. He knew about the Cobra. He knew about most stuff with me. But he didn't know about Courtney or my dumb little powers. No one did. And I liked that no one did.

I felt I could hold onto everything better if I never talked about it and nobody ever knew. As long as it stayed mine, it could still happen. It could.

Thank you, thank you.

Chapter 5

Mrs. Tracy clapped her hands together and everybody looked to the front of the class.

"I have two announcements to make," she said. "The first is something that worked very well last year in social studies, so I'd like to try it again with you."

"No tests?" said Rich. "Yay, no tests!"

"Funny, Rich, but no," Mrs. Tracy said. "I'm talking about having an election in class. Just like the real political elections coming up in a few weeks, in which I hope your parents will vote, I'd like to have a little mini-election right here. An election for classroom president."

Mrs. Tracy was beaming. I liked to see her excited. It was fun when she was really into something. She was tall and thin and not too old. Though she had been around for as long as I had been at St. Catherine's, she still seemed to get excited with each new class. I knew from the way seventh graders had talked about her in the past that she was the teacher to get, and it turned out to be true. Our first month in seventh grade had been one of the best so far.

"This is how it will work," she said. "For the next three weeks, we'll be learning about how governments work and what it means to hold public office. At the end of that time, we'll have a primary. That's when you can choose candidates from among yourselves. Everyone will have a chance to nominate someone they think would be best to lead the class in several activities we'll do this year."

"Can we nominate ourselves?" asked Joey Sisman.

"You better," said Jeff. "No one else will nominate you."

"Yes, we can nominate ourselves," Mrs. Tracy said, "though it would be nice if you offered your support to someone else in the class."

Joey pretended to nod thoughtfully. I heard Jeff chuckle quietly, probably because he got away with what he said.

"Once we decide on the candidates, we'll vote," Mrs. Tracy said. "The winner will be our classroom president. The first thing he or she will do is help me plan our Thanksgiving presentation for the parents. The president will form a committee for that. If this works out, we might have another election before Christmas for a new president. Maybe we'll do it every month. There's planning for our spring field trip, too."

"I would make sure we went to see a Broadway show, maybe *Phantom*," said Darlene, reminding everyone that she was Alice in last summer's peewee *Alice in Wonderland* and that she was taking professional singing lessons.

Mrs. Tracy smiled. "I'm sure that together we can think of a lot of good ideas to consider. And because of all the committees, everyone who wants to be involved can be. Trust me, every other class has loved this, and I'm sure it will be exciting and a lot of fun for you, too. It'll be a great way to learn about ourselves and the way people work together. . . ."

I glanced over at Courtney. She was looking up at the teacher, her pencil swaying back and forth between her fingers.

It was stupid, but I remember wondering right then if there might be something in this election, some way that things could happen, that would give me a way to do something she might notice. Maybe I couldn't exactly save her life, but . . . my mouth suddenly went dry.

No! Keep it to yourself! I thought.

But it was so easy, I couldn't keep it to myself. I got hot again under my blazer. Sweat rolled down inside my shirt.

I could nominate Courtney.

I could nominate her and then vote for her.

Wait, could I?

I could! It would seem so natural because she's so

incredible, who *wouldn't* nominate her. But if I nominated her it would move me to another whole level. I'd be "getting out there." And I'd finally be visible. Mostly, it would connect our names in class.

Mrs. Tracy, I'd like to nominate Courtney Zisky.

Me, Tom. Her, Courtney. She was so popular she would win, of course, and then she would say it:

Thank you, Tom.

Was it possible? Could it happen? Never mind the adventures for now. This was real. This was actually possible.

My heart was beating very fast. Courtney. Yes.

Ryan Ponacky said, "What's the second announcement?"

"No tests?" said Rich, trying his joke again and snickering quietly, but getting no laughs at all this time.

Mrs. Tracy glanced at the note on her desk. "Well, a new girl will be joining our class today," she said. "In just a few minutes, actually. Her name is Jessica Feeney."

Right away the class broke into a low buzzing noise.

"It's nice she's here for the elections," said Kayla, looking directly at Mrs. Tracy. "Right at the beginning, I mean."

Samantha Embriano raised her hand. "I'll show her around, and she can be my lunch buddy for a week — this week, okay?"

"I guess I'll take next week," said Eric LoBianco, a large boy who everyone said had wet his seat in second grade because the teacher wouldn't let him leave the class to use the bathroom. "Wait, is she good-looking?"

The girls in the room squealed and gagged.

Jeff laughed sharply. Rich howled.

A new girl?

I looked at Mrs. Tracy's face for some sign of what kind of person this girl might be. She had a cool name. Jessica. For an instant I wondered if she would be as pretty as Courtney. Just after I'd made all these plans about the election, wouldn't it be strange if a new girl came in smelling like peaches, too?

No way! Forget that. I nearly laughed out loud in my seat. No matter how good Jessica Feeney looked, no matter how nice she was, she'd never replace Courtney. A flash of Courtney in skiing clothes suddenly came into my mind. There was a distant echo of sniper shots in the white mountains behind her.

I smiled a little to myself. So that was it. I would nominate Courtney and vote for her. Then she'd know. It would be so cool.

It's odd now to think of how I almost missed what Mrs. Tracy said next. I almost missed it, thinking about Courtney, but I looked up just in time and now I can never forget it.

"There is . . . ," Mrs. Tracy was saying quietly, "there is something you need to know about Jessica. . . ."

Chapter 6

Mrs. Tracy held onto her smile, but it was clear that something really wasn't right about the whole second announcement. The pink was draining from her cheeks as she looked at us all. Then I noticed that she didn't so much look at us, as over and around us.

"Jessica," she said, "is a girl who has —" She stopped and looked at the door.

"What?" Kayla said softly behind me.

There was a tap at the door, and two or three kids in the middle of the room whispered and leaned forward to see out into the hallway. The door opened and the janitor walked in, sliding a desk noisily ahead of him.

"Where —" he said to no one in particular.

"In the back, please." Mrs. Tracy pointed to the end of the second row. The addition of another desk would make that row the longest.

"She's putting the new girl in the back of the room," Kayla whispered to me.

"I think I take back what I said," said Eric, just loud enough to be heard.

"Shh!" said Samantha Embriano.

The janitor scraped the desk along the floor between the first and second rows. I didn't like the way he did it; he could have carried it, after all. He set it at the end of the second row, spacing it perfectly from the desk in front of it with a flick of his wrist.

When he left, we all turned to Mrs. Tracy.

"Jessica has suffered a terrible thing," she said.

A couple of kids made noises. Their seats squeaked.

"Jessica was in a fire. She was burned, badly burned. She'll be going to school at St. Catherine's while she has treatments at a hospital in New Haven."

Some girl whispered "Oh" suddenly, and it sounded like she had hurt herself or something. We all looked, but the teacher went on.

"I don't know how long Jessica will be with us, but I want you to be prepared. Her burns are . . . she does not look like . . . anyone you have ever seen before. . . ."

Mrs. Tracy's voice caught and faded away for a second. Some of the kids seemed to get stiff in their seats. Others began shuffling things around on their desks. I felt nervous, as if I had been caught doing something wrong.

"But I know that you will treat her as good children should."

She stopped again. It was like a kind of wave passed over the class when she finished talking. I felt icy and weird in my stomach as if I was really hungry or really full. I kept on sweating and my forehead was damp, along with my waist.

It must be horrible, I thought.

If Mrs. Tracy talks like that, saying this girl was "badly burned," it must be horrible. And this girl is coming into our class? I remember thinking that as long as the teacher kept talking to us, even about a bad thing, the bad thing wouldn't happen yet because she had to tell us all about it before it happened. But now that Mrs. Tracy had said what she had said and stopped talking, there was nothing more between us and whatever it was that was waiting. Between us and Jessica Feeney.

I suddenly wished that while we were waiting, Mrs. Tracy would say something totally different, not about this girl, whoever she was. But about the weather. Or TV. Or the class elections. She should go through all that again. The primary. The voting. The committees. Thanksgiving. Anything to take our minds off of the whole "badly burned" thing she had just said.

I wanted to hear something, anything to assure us that even after this girl came into our class, things would still be normal and regular. I tried to imagine something about a volcano and a submarine, but I kept looking at Mrs. Tracy and nothing would come. She just twisted her hands for a while, then stopped, then waited, and then looked toward the hall.

Something was happening outside the door now.

This was it. The terrible thing was coming. Would somebody actually scream when they saw her, or say something? Would I say something? Would it be like a horror movie? A hideous creature? Or maybe it wouldn't be that bad?

My mother had burned herself at the stove lots of times. Just last week, in fact. The burns were red, sometimes a little white. But they weren't all that ugly. Maybe it wouldn't be that bad.

"We're not the closest school to the hospital," said Jeff, staring down at the top of his desk.

"What?" I looked over at him then back at the door. Mrs. Tracy moved to it, turning the knob.

It would be bad. I knew it would.

"We're a bunch of towns away; we're not the closest Catholic school for anybody to go to," said Jeff.

I watched the teacher open the door. Her left hand reached into the hall. She sort of half turned to the class. Her face was so pale then. Finally she said a bit more loudly than normal, "Class, I'd like you to welcome our new student."

She took the girl's hand and drew her in. "Everyone, say hello to Jessica."

As horrible as I thought the girl would look, when I imagined what burned people looked like, it was nothing compared to what stepped into the room.

Jessica Feeney's face, the first thing everyone looked at, was like a mask. I looked at her, then away, and then back at her. I couldn't believe I was looking at the face of someone alive.

The skin was all rough and uneven. It looked almost smeared and was stained all shades of pink and white and red.

Her lips were swollen. They nearly filled the space between her nose and chin. Her eyes peeked out from behind skin that looked melted. Her hair was mostly short. Her arms were covered, except that the forearms were bare and blotchy. Her fingers were bent as if she were trying to grab something.

My neck felt thick and stiff. There was a lump in my throat and a high ringing in my ears. I remember wondering how someone looking like that could even be alive. Was she in pain right now? It seemed like she must be. As if being in that skin would make you want to scream and scream and scream until you died.

But there was no screaming. It seemed like all the sound went out of the room for a long time while this girl stood there in front of us waiting. She stood stooped over in a brown dress. She had thick gray tights covering her legs. It wasn't the St. Catherine's uniform.

Finally, she said "Hi," in a small, tight voice, breaking the silence. Her mouth and cheeks hardly moved when she spoke. The skin on her throat was stretched and smeared like the rest of her. She's burned everywhere, I thought.

Someone whispered something and I felt my whole face go red. *Shut up. Everyone shut up. No, I mean talk! Fill the room up with noise. Be a regular class again now. Do it now!*

Mrs. Tracy seemed confused at first, but then said, "Will the people in row two please move back one seat each." Her face now was as white as I'd ever seen it. "Jessica, we sit alphabetically here, so your seat is at the head of row two."

"Okay," she whispered.

Without a word, Jeff collected his stuff and got up from his desk. So did the others. They moved back one seat. Everyone else tried to look busy as the new girl stood there waiting.

Finally, she sat down at her desk.

Jessica Feeney. The burned girl.

Without making much of a fuss, Mrs. Tracy went straight into science.

Chapter 7

"Well, that was fairly gross," said Jeff, hopping off the bus in front of me that afternoon. "The new girl." He made a noise like throwing up.

I thought of her face and felt my body go cold again. I wondered if I would ever forget what she looked like.

"Who'd want to be alive after that?" Jeff added, shaking his head as we crossed the yard. "The burns are all over her. Her hands are like claws, all bent up. Her fingers! Gross. Her fingers are totally stuck together. And you see the way she sits, bent over like that? All day I had to look at her. She's bent over because her skin is all tight, not like normal skin. It's all hard and crusty."

"Really?" I said. I wondered if that was true.

"I should know. My mother tells me about people like her from the hospital. It's the worst. Her skin must have melted on her, which means the fire was really, really hot. She was probably this close to dying."

We headed into the house and went to the basement.

"I just can't believe anybody could be alive after all that," I said.

"No kidding. The doctors probably kept her alive on tubes and stuff. I'd want to be dead. With a face like that, all, uck —"

We dropped onto the couches, and he started flipping through his comics, one after another. I could remember just about every detail of her face. It *was* like something melted, like wax on a candle. And all those, I don't know, *patches* of skin?

Flipping the pages but not reading, Jeff went on about her puffy arms and stringy hair and something he couldn't even bring himself to say, but just made noises about. I probably felt the same way he did, but it was starting to feel a little creepy talking out loud about it. I didn't want to hear it anymore. I found myself just blurting out the first thing I could think of.

"Yeah, well, she knows math, though."

He turned and looked at me, his face all screwed up. "Random much? What are you talking about? Math?"

"No, I mean she blows Kayla totally away in math," I said. "You can tell from that one answer she gave." So what *was* I talking about? Was I trying to sound all light and funny all of a sudden?

He snorted. "Who cares?"

I forced out a kind of chuckling sound and went on.

"But you know what the worst thing is? The worst thing is that you and me don't sit next to each other now. That's the real bummer. Mostly for you, though. You can't cheat off me."

"Uh-huh. What?" said Jeff. "I don't cheat. I never cheat. Hey, want to drive the Batmobile?"

Batmobile? Here it was again. The whole off-the-wall thing. He was already across the room, pulling the top box off a stack of cartons in the corner and rummaging in the one under it. All right, this was better. It was more like normal.

I played along. "Batmobile? What Batmobile?"

He pulled a radio-controlled model of Batman's black car from the carton. It had a lot of fins shooting off the back. A control box with toggle switches was attached to the car with a rubber band. He touched one of the toggles. It made a whirring sound, and he laughed.

"My stupid father got this for me a couple Christmases ago," he said, going for the stairs. "I can't believe the batteries still work."

I hated to hear him call his father that. Jeff was always mad whenever he talked about him. I started upstairs after him. "Cool. Can I drive it?"

"Let's set it on fire and burn it up. It'll get all drippy. Like her."

I felt as if someone had just poured ice water on me.

"Burn it? What do you mean burn it?"

Jeff flew up the stairs two at a time and through the kitchen. I followed, getting up to him just as a car door banged in the driveway.

"Your mother's home," I said. "Better not burn anything. . . ."

Jeff shrugged. "She doesn't care. Hey, Mom," he said, passing his mother on his way to the patio door. "We're going out back."

Mrs. Hicks stepped fully into the kitchen. She was wearing her light blue nurse's uniform. Now, at the end of her shift, the uniform was pretty wrinkled, but not bloody.

She didn't take any real notice of me standing there in the kitchen. Setting her pocketbook down on the table, she bent over to dig in it, her hair hanging down both sides of her face.

She sometimes works with burned people in her hospital in Bridgeport, I thought. I wonder if she knows anything about Jessica. Should I ask her?

Suddenly, she glanced up and caught me looking at her. I turned away and went to the backdoor where Jeff was waiting.

"Matches," she said sharply. "Jeff, have you seen any matches?"

He shrugged and shook his head a little. "Nah," he said, pushing out the door. "Tom, let's go."

We left her hunting through the cabinet drawers, one by one.

Once we were in the yard, Jeff dug his hand into his front pocket and pulled out a book of matches.

"You keep matches in your pocket?" I said. "Your mother was just looking for some."

He shrugged again. "It keeps her from smoking."

Setting the car on the ground, he put a match between the matchbook striking strip and the folded-over cover and whipped it out quickly. It snapped into flame.

"Jeff —" I said.

"Watch this," he said. He held the match under the car's front bumper. A few seconds later, the black plastic went orange as the flame grabbed it. It boiled slowly up the hood to the windscreen. The smell of burning plastic filled my nose. I arched back from it.

"It's just like that girl," Jeff said carelessly.

Enough, already. What a jerk. "You know, your mom's going to get mad. . . ."

"Look." Jumping up as the car's flame went higher, he pushed the control box's toggles down hard. On fire, the car skidded across the patio and over the slate walk, singeing the grass as it wheeled and bounced across the yard.

"What's amazing is how long it can keeping going, on fire," he said matter-of-factly, his thumbs working the levers.

The car spun through the leaves, darkening some where he slowed it, but mostly just trailing smoke above and behind it. He swung it around toward us, then zig-zagged it over the walk and onto the patio again. It bounced into the border on the edge of the stones.

In the border was a small rock that had a word carved on it — *dream.* The front passenger tire struck the rock. The car turned over and tumbled into the dirt. Flames wrapped around it, curling from the top to its underside, then going higher and filling the air with acrid, black smoke.

"Ahhh!" Jeff yelled in a mocking way. "The caped crusader is trying to escape, but he can't! He melts in flames! Robin, too! Yaaaah!" He laughed and laughed and jumped around the smoke.

The car was completely in flames now.

As suddenly as he started, Jeff seemed to get bored. He dropped the control box on the patio stones.

I couldn't stand to see the car on fire. It seemed stupid and a total waste. I turned around and picked up the garden hose, which was lying coiled on the edge of the patio. I sprayed the car. "I am The Spitter, helper of the dynamic duo!" I said, doing some stupid accent that made it sound like "Zee Spittaire!" I made a kind of laughing and spraying sound, as if it could all be part of Jeff's little car-burning game.

"That's so lame! What are you doing that for, for

Christ's sake?" Jeff cursed, jerking the water off. Then he kicked the car upright and cursed again. "Stupid."

I just stood there, holding the dripping hose.

"Jeff, get in here," his mother said. "Jeff." I smelled cigarette smoke coming from the kitchen.

He turned to go into the house, and then looked back. "Hey, did you know that my dad owns some original copies of *The Human Torch*? I think he left them in the attic. Let's go find them."

"But your mom —"

"Hey, did I ever tell you my uncle's coming?"

He dashed into the house while the smell of hose water and burning plastic drifted up over the patio.

Chapter 8

Over the next few days, mostly from things Mrs. Tracy said when Jessica Feeney wasn't there, which was a lot of the time, I picked up more stuff about her. One morning, I was in the hall near the classroom door when I overheard her telling one of the parents that Jessica and her family had been living in town for a week or two already. They had come down from Boston and were renting a condo really close to my house while she went for a bunch of tests and treatments at the hospital in New Haven.

"Jessica just finished undergoing some skin grafts," she said to Darlene's mother as I put my lunch in my locker. "Some more grafts," she added. "She's had quite a few already."

Undergoing was the word she used. She said it again to the class when Jessica was out of the room after lunch.

It sounded so creepy. I imagined someone lying flat on a table *going under* some kind of horrible machine.

After supper that night I searched the Net on my computer and found out basically that skin grafts are when doctors take skin from one part of a person and stick it on another part that is damaged, hoping it will grow normally. It seemed like some kind of horror story with bizarre people in wet basements doing things with bodies. I also found out that sometimes scientists grow stuff that looks and feels like skin. They make it in test tubes and then sew it onto where your skin is burned. Other times they take skin from an animal that's sort of pink, like a pig, and they use that on you, at least to start.

For faces, I read, it was mostly your own skin because it matched better, although Jessica's didn't really match much. It took time to heal, though, and then it blends better. They have pictures on the Internet that I didn't want to see, but I looked at anyway. They made me feel sick after eating so I stopped searching.

Just before bed, though, I was online again and I saw that there were long times between when burned people did the treatments — to see how well the skin grafts "took." I guessed they didn't go so well for Jessica and she was probably starting some more.

Somebody (I thought it might have been Courtney,

but I wasn't sure, because it made its way all across the room) said that Jessica's parents wanted her to keep up with Catholic school between hospital visits because she had lost almost a year of school time.

"Jessica's been to a number of hospitals over the last few months," Mrs. Tracy said, too. "So it's likely she won't be at St. Catherine's for very long. Though New Haven has, of course, one of the best hospitals, so there's really no telling."

The next day in the hall before lunch, I found myself telling Samantha Embriano and Joey that even though Jessica would normally have taken my bus in the morning, she didn't.

"When I was taking the absentee notes to the office this morning, I saw a man drive her in late," I said. "And yesterday afternoon, the same guy came early to pick her up."

"So that's her father?" said Samantha Embriano.

"I guess," I said.

"Does he look normal?" asked Joey.

I laughed. "What? Yeah. Of course!"

"So he wasn't in the fire?"

I felt a shiver run up my back. I'd never thought of that before. "No. I guess not."

When I came home after school on Wednesday, my mother was cutting vegetables at the kitchen counter. I dropped my backpack on the table and washed my hands.

She told me she heard from another mom that there was a new girl in my class.

I felt nervous all of a sudden. I had never said anything about Jessica, although she was pretty much all I was thinking about. I tried to be cool about it.

"Jessica Feeney," I said, wiping my hands dry.

"Right . . ."

I shrugged and didn't say much, not actually going to my room to start homework, but looking at the mail on the table and flipping through a clothes catalog that had come. I saw a picture of a girl who reminded me of Courtney. Then my mom started asking questions and I gave her some answers until somehow we were into what Jessica Feeney was like and I used the word *melted*.

My mother made a sound between her teeth.

I stopped. I never meant to say it; it just came out.

"I mean . . . not that," I said. "Just, you know —"

She was looking right at me now, her face drawing itself in like it does when she thinks something bad is happening to us.

"What?" I said. I didn't want to make too much out of it. All I wanted now was to get to my room and do homework.

"The poor girl. What is she like — I mean, is she — nice?"

"I don't know. I guess she's okay," I said, slinging my pack over my shoulder again. "She doesn't say much."

"She lives just over there." She pointed at the wall of the living room.

"I know." I stepped into the dining room. I was sweating again, and my shirt was wet and I wanted to change.

"Have you talked to her?"

"I don't know. It's school. There's stuff to do. Mrs. Tracy keeps us busy. Nobody talks to her much . . . there's stuff to do. . . ."

"Well, it might help to talk to her."

I think I squinted at her. "Help?" What did that mean? "I don't need help. I'm okay —"

"Her. Help her." She said this, shaking her head, as if she was going to say something more. But she didn't say anything else right then. I stood for another few seconds, then I went upstairs to change and do my homework.

After that first time in class on Monday, I had almost never looked right at Jessica Feeney. Not the next day or the next. It was really too hard to look at that face. It didn't get any better if you looked at it; I mean, it didn't get any easier to look at.

She answered the teacher's questions sometimes. Her voice was quiet and hoarse and not all that clear. She never raised her hand, but Mrs. Tracy called on her every now and again, and Jessica answered.

During math, she left her desk to sharpen her pencil. Sometimes she went into the hall to her locker and was gone in the lavatory for a while, then came back. She moved around all right, even though her legs were always covered with thick stockings. Maybe it hurt for her to move, but if it did, she didn't show it.

Then on Thursday of that week, a whole bunch of strange things happened.

I found that I started, in little bits, raising my head to look at her, but always when I knew she was turned the other way or couldn't see me. I discovered that if you didn't see the edge of her face or her hand or arm lying on the desk, she looked almost like any girl with dirty hair. It was sort of crushed and matted in the back. It almost began to feel as if there was a person in there.

As if there was a person in there. It seems stupid to even say something like that. But that's what I felt. It was hard to think about her as being at all like the rest of us.

Still, I remember letting out a deep breath the first time I found myself looking at her from behind. It was as if I had been holding my breath ever since she stepped into our class. When she was turned away, you could almost forget about the way she looked. It almost didn't matter that Jessica Feeney, the horribly burned girl, was sitting one seat away from me at the head of row two.

Jeff, on the other hand, and Rich, were acting as if there was something else to know about Jessica.

There was, they said, the whole question of *how.*

Chapter 9

It was hot outside when I trotted across the yard in gym class and heard Jeff say, "How did she get that way?"

"Yeah, how?" said Rich, who was standing with him. The look on his face showed that he'd been wondering things aloud, too.

"So what burned her?" Jeff said to us. "That's what I want to know. Nobody's talking about it. How it happened. That's the point."

The point?

"Somebody must know," said Rich, his eyes darting around and his head nodding quickly, as if no one could possibly disagree with that. "Mrs. Tracy knows for sure."

Jeff snorted. "Why don't you go ask her?" he said. He gave Rich a hard push toward the school. "Then go do a report on it."

"I'm not going to ask her!"

"Why not, you love Mrs. Tracy. You want to kiss her —"

"I do not!"

I was moving from one foot to the other as I listened to them talking. It surprised me that with everything going on during Jessica's first week at St. Catherine's, I hadn't even thought of that part of the situation. It suddenly seemed really odd to me that I never even asked myself how. I mean, of course, right? How did she get burned? How did it happen? How could she be like that?

"It was probably in her house," Rich said. "She was playing with matches and the curtains caught fire or something. That's what I think. When I was three I supposedly lit a tablecloth on fire. It was Thanksgiving and I was under the table —"

"She was burned about two years ago, maybe two and a half," said Jeff as if he was certain. "From what my mother says, that's what you look like. She should have died. That's about as bad as you can get and still live —"

"You talked to your mother about her?" I asked.

"Plus, she's big," he went on, "so she's probably a couple of years older than us. She must have been in the hospital for a long time after she got burned and lost at least a year of school. Maybe more."

"You know a lot," said Rich, almost in awe.

Now I couldn't get it out of my mind. Jessica's face

came to me again and I must have begun to wince or something because Rich laughed and pointed at me. I turned away from him. But I did begin to wonder why Mrs. Tracy hadn't said something like, "don't play with matches," or "don't stick things in electrical sockets," or "don't fool around in the kitchen," using Jessica as a sort of warning of what could happen.

"Maybe it was just an accident?" I said.

Jeff made a noise under his breath. "Yeah. Maybe. Or maybe it was something else."

"That's what I think," said Rich, as if what Jeff had just said really meant anything. "Plus, I wonder if anybody else was in the fire and then died."

Jeff nodded slowly. "Sure, probably. That bad? Oh, yeah."

Some girls, Courtney and Darlene and someone else, were beginning to shoot hoops across the yard, and the coach, Mrs. Brower, turned toward us, her whistle between her teeth. The necklace of the whistle strap looped behind her neck.

"She's going to call us now," I said.

"Joey said he saw her father, but he's mostly normal, not all burned up like she is," Rich whispered.

I felt my face go red, and I turned to Jeff. "Joey didn't see her father, I saw him. And of course he's normal —"

"Maybe her mother, then," said Jeff.

For the second time, I felt as if I wanted to shove this conversation aside somehow, wreck it. It seemed so dumb to stand around wondering about how somebody got the way she was. It happened. So, okay. Why talk about it? I wanted to walk away from them, but I didn't. I wondered why I didn't, but I wasn't sure. I was hoping Mrs. Brower would finally call us to do something, but she was still across the yard, talking to some of the girls and moving her arms.

"Or a dog?" said Rich, his eyes large. "Maybe her dog died. Pets stay with you in a fire I heard —"

"Anyway," I said, interrupting loudly, not wanting to talk about pets and fires anymore. "Jeff, how about when we go driving around next Saturday, you know —"

"Huh?" He turned to me, narrowing his eyes as if he wasn't getting it. "You say the queerest things. What are you talking about?"

"I was thinking that . . . uh . . ." I didn't know why I said what I said next, but it just came out. "Maybe we can drive by Courtney's house. We can go by her house and honk the horn."

I couldn't believe what I was saying. My pulse was racing hard. My voice was quivering. My chest thumped. What's this? Why this? Courtney? I'm saying her name? Here? I'm giving up my secret? Why? For her? For Jessica Feeney? So we wouldn't talk about her anymore?

Jeff looked at me. His face was a blank.

"I mean, your uncle's still coming over next weekend, right?" I asked.

"What are you talking about?" said Rich, looking back and forth between us. "What uncle?"

Jeff nodded. "He's coming."

"And he'll have the you-know-what?"

"What you-know-what?" asked Rich.

"You know," I said, not taking my eyes off Jeff.

Finally he grinned back. "Yeah . . . yeah . . . Courtney's house," he said, glancing at Rich, who was still in the dark. "Yeah. Cool."

But for some reason, that wasn't enough to push it away. Rich already seemed bored with our talk. When he looked once more back at the school, he had a smirky little smile on his face. It seemed as if he was remembering some other thing he had heard about Jessica, and it wasn't going to be nice.

"I'm going to nominate Courtney, too," I blurted out, spilling everything right there on the gym yard. Some idiot in my brain kept saying *go on, tell them everything, tell them all about it, you jerk!*

"I'm going to do it first," I said, "before anybody else has a chance."

The coach was finally coming toward us now. I heard one of her knees snapping loudly as she walked.

Rich still had that face on. He was going to say something. His mouth opened. "And you know what else —"

I had to finish it. It was complete idiocy. "I really like her," I said quickly. "I like Courtney. She'd make a cool president."

Rich's face grew suddenly huge. "What? You love her?" His eyes went wide, his mouth dropped open exaggeratedly. "Tom loves Courtney. Oooh! Jeff, he loves Courtney! Oooh, *Tah-om* —"

"She's gonna win," Jeff said quietly as Mrs. Brower finally blew her whistle. The class started, and we were pulled apart to different sides of the yard.

Everything was a blur during the rest of gym class. I couldn't believe that I had just told them everything. I had told them I liked Courtney!

Later, just before lunch, when it was time for social studies, Mrs. Tracy clasped her hands together and looked around to get everyone's attention.

"Another announcement?" someone whispered from the back. "Not another new person!"

That was a pretty stupid thing to say.

"Before we start social studies," Mrs. Tracy said, "Sister Margaret Christopher has suggested that the classes join in a special prayer for all the candidates in the real elections this year. A prayer that they may make the right decisions and will guide us and help us lead safe and prosperous lives in our state and our country. All the grades are doing it. So, hands, everyone."

"Hold hands? No way," said Eric LoBianco, repeating what he said every prayer time.

"It's a short prayer," Mrs. Tracy said, looking at Eric. "And we will all participate. The more of us who say the prayer, the better the chance it will be heard."

Kayla made a show of wiping her small hands, then held them out, one to Rich and the other to me.

I glanced to the back corner to see Courtney holding Dave Tessman's hand. I wondered for an instant if Dave felt anything for Courtney or knew how lucky he was. His other hand held his twin sister Karen's hand. Dave and Karen Tessman.

As everyone reached out, something rippled across the room, as if they all suddenly thought of the same thing at the same time: Jessica Feeney was in the class now.

Coming in late and leaving early most days, she had always missed the morning and afternoon prayer rings. But now she was here. This was the first time her burned hands would be part of the prayer ring.

She stood up and extended her hand to me.

I felt as if everyone's eyes were on me. I must have dropped a gallon of sweat into my shirt. I felt my arms and sides and waist dripping wet. But with that curled thing held out in the air toward me, I couldn't not take it. I had to hold it. My hand reached out to hers and took it.

I held it lightly, and I think she helped by not squeezing. My hand must have been sweaty. Her palm felt pretty normal. The skin felt cool.

It's not the burned side, I told myself.

Of course. She must have kept her hands all fisted up when she was in the fire, banging whatever it was to get out of wherever she was when the fire was all around her.

When she turned to Jeff, he kept his eyes down and his arms down. She extended her hand, crooked and red and bent open, but he made no move. Everyone stood there, completely silent and waiting.

"Jeff," said Mrs. Tracy, glancing over at him with a frown and eyes that were stern and dark. Her head was half-bowed to begin the prayer.

Jeff did not meet her look. He set his feet firmly on the floor, legs apart as if he expected a huge wave or something to wash over him. He pushed his balled-up fists into his pockets and didn't hold anyone's hand. He looked ready to leave the classroom any second.

"It's okay," said Jessica, letting her hand drop.

Mrs. Tracy closed her eyes and said the prayer.

Chapter 10

"I can't believe you did that," Rich said to Jeff at lunch.

"You're in trouble," said Joey. "You can't just *not* do what Mrs. Tracy says you have to. Especially not a prayer thing. The nuns will get on your case. It's at least detention for sure."

Jeff shrugged, dropping his brown bag on the table. "I'm not touching that girl," he said coolly. "My mom's a nurse. You think she doesn't know how you can pick up diseases and stuff from touching sick people? She tells me all kinds of stories."

"You mean like AIDS?" asked Rich. "Whoa."

I stared at my sandwich. My heart was beating hard. "Like AIDS? It's not like she's contagious or anything —"

"Oh, what, like you know?" said Joey, looking at Jeff.

"She's not still burning —" I said.

"You're lucky," said Jeff, pulling a piece of his

sandwich off and pushing it into his mouth. "You don't have to stare at the back of her head all day."

"She looks like everybody else from behind," I said.

Rich shook his head, looking at Jeff now, too. "Not really, right?"

"It's like I can see her skull through her burned hair," said Jeff, more angry now. "And her smell is making me sick. I should ask to move my seat. I've already pushed it back a lot. But not enough. I've got to move my seat."

I glanced around the cafeteria but didn't see Jessica. It struck me that I had never seen her there. Where did she eat?

"In fact, I'm going to talk to Mrs. Tracy now," he said. He got up from the table with his bag in his hand. "Where is she? I'll get her to move my seat. My mom will call her if I tell her to."

I watched Jeff storm away from the table and out into the hall.

After lunch, Mrs. Tracy started teaching English without saying a word about the handholding thing. I kept expecting her to say something or give Jeff harsh looks, but she never did.

And Jeff, who stayed where he was in row two but moved his seat only another few inches back, didn't seem worried about getting punished, either, as Joey had warned he might.

Had he already talked with Mrs. Tracy? Did he

actually convince her that there was some danger in being near Jessica or touching her? Did he tell her his mother would call the school? That was just crazy.

But Mrs. Tracy said nothing at all about it. She began by reading a poem about Chicago, one about trains, and then another about Abraham Lincoln.

The whole afternoon, Jessica's head was almost always bent down over her books. In fact, she hardly looked up for the rest of the day. I knew because I found myself watching her a lot.

Jessica was absent the next day, Friday. For treatment, Mrs. Tracy said. Jeff wasn't there, either. He had gone for a long weekend to visit his father, who lived in New York with his girlfriend.

I was amazed at how relieved I was that neither of them was there. Friday was great. I could just do my work. I had felt so sick to my stomach the day before from the talk on the school yard and the prayer ring. But Friday turned out really good.

At lunch I sat alone and did some catch-up homework. Rich, Joey, and Eric were two tables away making faces and waving their hands about some show they had seen the night before. Courtney, Darlene, and Kayla were running around with some of the kindergartners doing something I didn't know about. That was all fine. It was the usual, and I liked it.

A big chunk of the class time was taken up talking

about and doing stuff for the elections. Mrs. Tracy said we would have our primary to choose candidates in a little over two weeks, so we had to get into high gear if we wanted to get everything done in time. That was fine with me. It felt like regular school again.

I didn't see Jeff until the morning bus on Monday. He was waiting at the stop. He seemed more or less okay, but quiet.

"So, how was your weekend in New York?" I asked him.

He shrugged. "My dad gave me some of his stupid old comics. I don't even know why he has them there, but his girlfriend wanted them out. That's pretty much it."

"Yeah. What kind of stuff did you do —"

"I never do anything there," he snapped, finally looking at me. "The guy can't wait for the weekend to be over and for me to be gone."

"Really? Sorry," I said.

He looked past me up the street to where the bus would come from. "We're supposed to do all kinds of stuff. It's supposed to be different when I go there. But all he wants is to go places with his girlfriend. The jerk."

"What, they do stuff alone?" I asked. "What do you do?"

"Nothing. I just wait. Plus, they live in this really tiny place. It's such a waste."

When the bus finally came, he stomped up the steps

and slumped into a seat. I sat down next to him, but he just stared out the window. I wanted to ask about the car again, but bringing up his uncle didn't feel right just then. When the bus was weaving around the streets near school, he suddenly ripped out a piece of loose-leaf paper and began to scrawl something on it. Then he balled it up and threw it to the floor under the seat. "Jerk," he said a few times.

He jumped off the bus, pretty much just stormed to the classroom, and slapped his notebooks down on his desk. Jessica wasn't there yet. Our bus must have been first because Courtney wasn't there, either.

Shaking his head, Jeff looked over at me again. "I mean, Deb, his girlfriend, is okay. But so what? You wouldn't believe the tiny, tiny place they have. I have to sleep on the couch with my feet practically in the oven. Plus, it stinks of bug spray. He keeps saying it's all he can get because my mother is forcing him to pay for school for me, and I should go to public school instead. He says I would probably even like it better. When I got home last night my mother was on emergency shift anyway. I didn't see her till this morning. So she's not even there, either. So who even cares?"

Jeff let all his breath out.

It sounded really horrible for him. I couldn't picture it all because things were okay at my house. It was like trying to understand what it felt like to have cancer or something. I didn't know. I couldn't know. But it seemed like after every visit, he hated his father more and more. It made me feel guilty that I had both my parents. "Sorry it stinks so much," I said. "You could come to my house after school maybe. There's food at least."

He shook his head. "My mom always leaves me food. She just works a lot. Plus, you don't have any good stuff. The only comics you have are the ones I gave you."

It still seemed so incredibly dumb to talk about cars when he was having such a bad time at home, so I just said, "Yeah, you have better stuff."

Class started, and Jessica came in twenty minutes later. She was quiet and stayed to herself as usual. Since it was now only two weeks before the actual election, the whole project began to take up more and more class time. The day started with a half period of what Mrs. Tracy called the "background" part of the project. Talking the whole time, Samantha Embriano and Kayla tacked their extra-credit poster project about primaries to the bulletin board. It was drawn with lots of different colored markers. Right after them, Darlene marched up with a better one, a flowchart with little orange Halloween lights fitted through the poster board. The lights showed how candidates for an office start up a campaign, how they raise money, how they get nominated, and how elections are done.

Mrs. Tracy wouldn't allow us to campaign for class

president until the end of each day, when we could get up and present five-minute speeches about ourselves. But Darlene, at least, started right from the beginning. She wore a homemade "Darlene" button every day, and she brought in brownies for lunch two days in a row. "Just because," she said. "The ones with nuts are marked with a nut on top. The others are plain."

Eric LoBianco came in on Wednesday with his own plate of cookies. He said he baked them himself, which Darlene didn't believe. When the cookies were found to not be very good, Ryan said it was probably true that he made them after all.

Finally, it was time for the speeches and the real election posters to come out. Mrs. Tracy wanted everybody to do something, but not everyone did. Some kids just didn't want to run and said so. I didn't want to run for anything, but I didn't say so because no one asked, so I just watched and listened.

Karen talked about write-in candidates, which is when the person who votes can write in the name of someone who hasn't been officially nominated. It was a dual presentation with Melissa. They were thinking of running together as co-presidents, and Mrs. Tracy said that was okay, for now.

At the very end of the day on Wednesday, Courtney gave her talk. I listened to every word. She spoke the same way she did at the reading group, her voice going high and low. She looked at index cards some of the time, but didn't for quite a bit of it. She told us about how the people who hold office really need to listen to the people they represent, even if they don't say much. She said that listening was what being elected to a position was really all about.

"It's the heart of the democratic process," she finished.

When she said *heart* I think I shivered. Her face did a little frown when she prounounced the word, as if she meant everything the word could mean. She looked out at the whole class but at no one in particular when she said it. Then she nodded once and sat down.

Jessica was out that day and the day before. I thought at first that she went into the hospital for more graftings, but then I thought that maybe she just had a cold or wasn't feeling well or something. Mrs. Tracy didn't say why.

Mostly because my mother kept at me to get out there and get involved, even though I didn't want to, that night I made a small poster with my name stenciled under a blown-up photocopy of my last year's school picture.

We were all around the kitchen table after dinner on Wednesday night looking at it.

My mother frowned. "It needs more."

"It needs somebody else," I said.

"Just a little pizzazz," she said, making a face at me.

We were all thinking of things, when my father's eyes lit up.

He sat upright in his chair, a smile growing on his face. "I've got it," he said. Then, not to me, but to my mother he said, "A vote for Tom is a vote for tomorrow. Except that the t-o-m of tomorrow is capitalized. So that it reads —" He moved his hands over the poster on the table in front of us. "A Vote for Tom is a Vote for TOM-orrow. Get it?"

He looked at me now.

I looked at my mother. "What?" I said.

"That's good," said my mother.

A few minutes later, the poster was done.

A Vote for TOM is a Vote for TOMorrow!

I didn't like the slogan. I didn't like it because I wasn't sure exactly what it meant. How do you vote for tomorrow? What would a vote for tomorrow look like? Isn't tomorrow just a big question mark? They always say tomorrow never comes, right?

The more I thought about it, the more I believed the slogan might mean nothing at all. And after Courtney talked about the whole democratic process thing, and frowned when she said *heart,* how could I put up a poster that didn't mean anything?

I looked at it in my room later, propped up against my backpack and ready for school.

"Tom . . . T-O-M," I said. "Get it?"

That night, as I lay in the dark, I kept replaying the scene where Courtney would look at the poster and frown.

"What does it mean?" she would ask me seriously.

My mind would go completely blank. Then I would suddenly stare past her to the end of the hall, where the tiles began popping up out of the floor.

My father stopped me on the stairs the next afternoon. "How do your friends like your poster?" he asked.

"They love it," I said. "It's funny, but also true."

He seemed to like that. "Did you do your talk yet?"

"Tomorrow, I think."

The idea was that I would talk about how politicians were in office for two or four or six years and were supposed to leave office with things better than when they got elected. If politicians kept doing that, the world would really become a better place.

I felt bad, but there was no way I was going to talk in front of the class, and I sure didn't want to show the poster to anybody, not even Jeff. I had already decided to keep it in my locker until after the election.

In the meantime, Joey Sisman kept threatening to nominate himself if no one else did and vote for himself, too.

On Friday morning, Jessica came in just after prayers. I think she timed coming in so she wouldn't have to be there for that. The day was a warm one again, and while I helped Mrs. Tracy hook the window pole on the latch of one of the upper windows, wondering whether tomorrow was going to be sunny, too, I thought I saw Courtney and Jessica talk to each other when Courtney was handing back papers. I remember I felt all nervous in my chest and guilty, as if I'd done something wrong again and was going to be found out.

They probably just said a couple of words, like "here you go" and "thanks," but it made me think that even though she'd been there for two weeks already, no one had really said much to Jessica. What I'd told my mother the week before was still true.

I hated it, but everyone (the whole class and me, too) seemed happier the days she wasn't there.

Then, in the three minutes between subjects on Friday morning, while Mrs. Tracy was chatting in the hallway with another teacher, something else happened.

Chapter 11

As everyone put their religion books away and got out
calculators and pencils for math, Jessica reached under
her seat for her pencil case. Her fingers fumbled a bit in
it, and as she leaned over to peer into the case, a pencil
and a photograph fell out of it. The photo landed face up
near the foot of my desk.

"Oh," she said. She reached for it, but it was nearer
to me.

I lifted the picture from the floor. It was an odd size,
almost exactly square. It was a picture of a girl. She was
short and pretty and blonde and looking straight into the
camera. Propped on her left shoulder was a tennis racket.
Behind her stood a man in a white sweater and shorts.
He had a big smile on his face. Squarely behind them
both was a big shingled building that looked like a fancy
beach club in the summer. The right side of the photo,

next to the man, was clipped off. But my eyes were drawn to the girl.

Her eyebrows were cocked at a slight angle, and her eyes were big and beautiful. Her lips were half-curved in a little, cute smile.

"Who's she?" I found myself asking at the same time a shiver went right up my back. For a split second it occurred to me that the picture might actually be of her.

That girl might be Jessica.

Idiot! How could I blurt out, *"Who's she?"*

I began to feel really nervous again, but I tried to make it pass. It couldn't be her. This girl was smaller, much smaller. With my hand trembling, I started to give it back.

But Kayla stopped me, practically lunging at my hand and stopping it. "Oh, my gosh," she whispered. "Is that her?"

Her? My stomach began to roll now, and I thought I was going to be sick all over the place. You idiot. Jessica's right here!

"Here," I said, trying to hand it back again, but Kayla wouldn't let go of my wrist. It was insane. This little girl was holding onto me. Mrs. Tracy was talking intently with Darlene and Dave now, and then began digging in the bookshelves under the window and didn't notice what was going on. Samantha Embriano suddenly rose from her desk to look at the picture now. Rich Downing was sliding out of his seat, too.

"Hey, that's the guy that picks you up!" said Rich, pointing his finger at the man in the picture, but at least talking to Jessica. "That's your father isn't it?"

Jessica said nothing, so I said, "Maybe. Here." I still tried to move my hand.

"It's my sister," said Jessica quietly, reaching for the photo. "That's my sister. Anne."

We were all quiet. Her sister? That was the first we'd heard about a sister. Not that we ever asked or anything.

"Anne," said Kayla. "Cool."

Samantha Embriano suddenly said something completely out of nowhere, but it was kind of good. "I used to play tennis. That's a good racket she's got there. You can tell from the *P* on the face of it —" She practically touched the photograph. "I know, because my tennis teacher has one like that."

"You have a tennis teacher?" Rich asked.

"Since third grade," she said.

"Your sister's really cute," said Kayla, finally releasing my hand.

Her sister. Anne. I don't know what Jessica thought about all this. Since we were all bunched so close together it was impossible to look at her without seeming to stare into her face. Plus her head was down, so it was hard to figure out what she was thinking.

But I know what I was thinking. I was thinking that she probably couldn't believe any of this. I couldn't believe it! All these words at once. It was more than anyone had spoken to her since she came to our class. So many words!

And I knew why.

We had all been waiting so long for things to be more normal again. It was what everybody felt when Jessica wasn't in school for a day. Only this was a hundred times better. We didn't have to pretend she didn't exist. We suddenly found a regular thing about her — her sister.

Her sister wasn't burned. Anne was a normal girl. A really cute girl, in fact. And now that we saw this picture and we knew about her, we had found out another thing about Jessica . . . lots of things, in fact — normal things that we could think about and talk about. Tennis. The beach club. Summer vacation. Their father. About anything. It was as if someone had opened a window in a hot room and cool air was rushing in over us.

Jessica hadn't moved during all of this and said nothing, but I almost felt happy for her. Wouldn't it be so much easier this way? We could show that we could be friends with Jessica by being interested in her sister. This was it. We could almost be normal again.

"Cool," I said, reaching over to give the photo back.

Suddenly it was Rich's turn to be the idiot. He said something so incredibly simple, but right away everything I had just been thinking began to fall apart.

"She looks like she's maybe in fifth grade," he said. "Is she in one of the downstairs classes?"

It was quiet for a moment. Everyone was quiet, waiting for her to answer. Out of the corner of my eye, I saw Jeff sitting facing away from us, his legs sticking out between the second and third rows.

Then Kayla asked, "Does she have Mr. MacDonald? My brother would know her."

I gave Jessica the picture back finally. When I did, her hand sort of brushed against mine. It was rough. A jolt of something electric went straight down my back to my legs. It felt as if a skeleton had just tapped my shoulder.

She put the photo back in her pencil case, and then gripped the zipper with her thumb and first finger and pulled.

"Is she in his class?" Kayla asked, looking at each of us.

"She's not here," said Jessica. Her voice was unsteady.

I felt cold again. Seeing Jessica fumbling to close the pencil case, I just wanted the questions to stop now. But everybody was looking at her. When Rich spoke again, it was the end of it.

"Where is she?" he asked, glancing over at Jeff who was still leaning back, saying nothing.

Jessica pulled the zipper closed. "She died."

The words were almost inaudible, but it felt as if all the air was pulled out of me when she said them.

Without waiting, she stood up and went to the teacher and said something to her.

"Hey, wait a minute," Rich said to us. "That's not fair. I didn't do anything wrong. I just asked her where she was. I didn't know anybody was dead. Who cares if her dumb sister's dead? She better not say anything about me —"

But nothing happened. Mrs. Tracy didn't even look over at Rich or Kayla or me or the others going back to their seats.

It was like it didn't involve us. Mrs. Tracy nodded, and Jessica left the classroom.

Chapter 12

It was everywhere by the end of lunch . . . that Jessica Feeney had started a fire in her room while playing with matches and that's how she got burned; but worse than that, the fire had killed her sister. And the reason why Jessica had to enter school after the year started was because people found out she killed her sister and they made her leave the town she lived in before.

It was totally bizarre. And it probably wasn't even possible. People didn't get thrown out of their towns anymore. That was something they did in the Old West or in Frankenstein movies. People with torches marching to your house.

Meanwhile, I found that all I could think about, all I could wonder about, was what Jessica looked like before.

If her sister was so cute, was *she* cute, too? It was hard to get straight in my mind exactly what she might look like. When I thought about all the stuff I had dreamed up about Courtney, I realized that most of it was because of how beautiful she was. But what if Jessica was like that, too? I couldn't hold it in my head without feeling like I was going to cry.

But the talk kept up all afternoon.

After lunch, the class split up into French and Spanish language sections in different rooms, and by the time we all got back together in our right seats, the story seemed to have gone through ten more versions with every new off-the-wall idea added into the mess.

Now there were curtains involved, and candles, and matches, a dog (who also died), a curse whispered on the prettier sister, and a big flowery tablecloth — with blood stains.

It was as if everybody's worst fears about why Jessica looked the way she did were suddenly turned loose, and it was okay to say them. It was okay now because the fire had all been her fault. What started as a real possibility for us to be normal again turned into a nightmare.

The big turning point — all that talk I had hoped for when I first saw the photo — had come, all right. But it was all wrong. I had wanted it to be about tennis and beach clubs and summer, but by last period it had turned into a freaky murder story.

In some versions of it, Jessica and her (now) genius sister had had an argument — some people said over a boyfriend, some said over dolls — then Jessica got mad and set the dolls on fire. Her sister didn't make it out of the house (neither did the dog), and Jessica was saved only because the firemen chopped through the walls to get to her.

Which they probably shouldn't have, someone said.

And now her family had to keep moving because she was running from the police, who suspected the real story and were close to proving it.

"That's why she cut herself out of the photo," said Eric LoBianco in the lavatory before health class. "So the police couldn't use it to identify her."

I sighed. "That's the dumbest thing I ever heard. Jessica's at our school because she has to go where the good burn hospitals are."

"That's what she says —"

"Like New Haven," I said. "And how is she running from the police if she's in school where everybody can see her?"

Ignoring that, Eric said, "Feeney sort of sounds like a made-up name, doesn't it? Jessica Feeney? Jessica Phony, more like it."

The sound of Rich's laughter came from inside a stall just before the toilet flushed. "Jessica Phony Baloney!"

"No, wait, you guys," I said, my throat suddenly hot. "Nobody knows —" I wanted to say that nobody even knew what happened. It was just a picture of her sister that started all the rumors. But I wasn't sure what I was trying to say and I couldn't seem to get it out right.

"Maybe we should call the police," said Joey Sisman, back in the classroom, where we set up the AV equipment for health. "Tell them that she's right here in our school. She left today because we found out her secret, but maybe they can send cars and catch her before she moves."

"We should at least tell Mrs. Tracy that we're afraid," Kayla suggested. "I mean, I guess we're scared, right?"

"Scared?" I said. "You're scared?"

"I'm not scared," said Eric.

"Me, either," Rich added, puffing himself up. "I can handle killers okay. Except don't make me touch them."

The afternoon just dragged on and on. The worst of it came when someone said that Jessica should be the dead one, and not her innocent, kind, TV-beautiful, tennis-playing genius of a sister.

I felt so mad. I was really mad. What people were saying was all so idiotic and pointless and hurtful that it made me sick. I tried lots of times to say something, but it sounded just as lame as the things they were saying. "Nobody knows what happened! It's just a picture!" I finally nearly asked to go to the nurse.

I only stayed because the day was almost over anyway, and I didn't want to miss any work. And it wasn't everybody. It was actually just a few kids, and some of them, like Kayla, didn't think anything was real. They just wondered if this was true or that was true. I must have said it was dumb to Joey and Ryan and Rich about a thousand times before the end of the day. Finally, I just stopped. I didn't like the feeling of being the only one and alone, like she was alone. That wasn't fair, either. By last period, it had almost died down anyway.

Jeff had been pretty quiet the whole afternoon. The Cobra thing was supposed to happen the next day, but he hadn't said a word about it all week, so I wasn't sure his uncle was even coming. Then, while we were packing up our books to go home, but before the buses were called, he turned to me.

"Maybe I should go to public school," he said.

I wondered if he was doing that thing again. "What do you mean?" I asked.

"My father would sure be happy," he said. "And my mom would probably get off my case about grades." He looked right at me with a face that seemed cold. "Besides, if I did go to public school, I wouldn't have to be here and see her and all this —"

He swore under his breath.

Even though he didn't mention the fire or the supposed murder, a spike of something jolted through me. He was really close to being mean about Jessica again, and I didn't want to hear it.

"Is your uncle coming over tomorrow?" I asked, trying not to make it seem like a big deal. "You said he was, right?"

He shook his head. "Nah. Next week for sure. I gotta go to my father's dump again. My mom's working the whole long weekend. Can you believe it?"

That's right. It was Columbus Day on Monday. My family always took a long car ride and looked for pumpkins up in the country. "That stinks," I said. I shrugged a little and tried not to make it any worse. I knew something was going on.

"Here's *The Human Torch*," he said, digging into his backpack, then holding up four or five comics. "I thought they'd be better from the way my dad talked about them. Anyway, they're only okay. This one's the best. You can have them. I have some more at home, too. I don't have to go to the city until morning. You coming over now?"

I took the comics but didn't feel like going. I was tired and didn't want to hear Jeff say anything about Jessica, and then find myself laughing five minutes later at some doofus thing he did.

"I can't," I said, trying to think of something. "I've sort of got stuff to do. . . . I have this church thing of my mom's after school. She signed me up to help."

"Are you kidding? What are you going to do there?"

I shrugged. "I don't even know."

When they started calling buses, and Jeff went into

the hall to his locker along with some other kids, Mrs. Tracy called me up to her desk.

"Would you please take Jessica's homework to her?" she said. "And her math book? She left before I remembered to send the assignments home with her. I want her to have them for the long weekend."

Talk about off-the-wall. I guess I looked surprised. "What?"

"You're just a few houses away from where she lives, aren't you?" she asked, waiting. "Or are you busy after school? Do you have something to do?"

I couldn't tell her the church thing because she'd know there was no church thing. "Um . . . okay," I said finally. "I mean no, I don't think I have anything. I guess I can take it."

"Great. Would you find her math book while I write a note?" She sat down to write while I went to Jessica's desk and reached under the seat.

"You're taking stuff to Jessica?"

I looked up. It was Courtney. She had paused on her way to the lockers.

I was surprised. "Yeah. I live nearby."

"Right," she said. "Nice."

Nice? What was this? And right? Did Courtney even know where I lived?

"Don't forget the workbook," she added.

"Oh, yeah. Thanks." I dug out the math book and the

workbook underneath it. When I looked up, Courtney had already gone. Jeff was standing there instead.

"Church thing, huh?"

"Well, yeah, but Mrs. Tracy . . ." I wanted to say something more, but Jeff turned and went straight back into the hall. The office secretary announced our bus over the PA and I got Mrs. Tracy's note and quickly followed everybody out.

Chapter 13

On the bus, Jeff swung into a seat up front that already had someone sitting by the window. I went to our usual seat in the back. When his stop came, he ran off to his house without looking back. One stop later, I got off and headed straight to the condo development where Jessica lived.

It was small, as developments go; just five houses tucked into what were probably originally people's backyards. Each house was divided into two side-by-side units with two different families living in them.

As I approached number seven, I noticed a man standing in the side doorway near the garage. He was dressed in a flannel shirt and was reaching up inside over the door, moving his arm from side to side. It was the man in the picture who I had seen taking Jessica to and from school.

When he lowered his hand, which had a wet rag in it, he also lowered his eyes and saw me.

"Yes?" he said, holding the rag still, and looking through the door screen with a blank expression.

"I just came to give her her homework," I said.

The guy looked at me.

"Jessica, I mean. I have her homework."

He kept just looking.

"It's because she left school early today," I said. "So the teacher said because I live not too far away I should give her the assignments. And these books." I lifted my arm slightly to show the books. Finally, I added, "My name is Tom Bender."

Another moment of staring, then the man relaxed. "Oh, right, sure. Sorry, I'm Jessica's father. Of course. Who else would I be? Come on in. Careful of the bucket."

He swung open the screen and I stepped into a small hall off the kitchen. There were dishes stacked in the sink and on the table. They were caked with the remains of some kind of hardened green vegetable and dried ketchup.

"I wasn't expecting anyone," Mr. Feeney said in a tired voice. Still holding his rag, he took me through the kitchen and dining room to the stairs and stopped. "Jessica —"

Suddenly, there she was, coming round the corner of the living room and nearly bumping into us.

"Oh!" she whispered.

She looked right at me with her face right there.

I felt as if I must have leaped back a foot. I was ashamed at how it probably looked. Somehow I managed a smile and said, "Sorry, you scared me."

That didn't sound right.

"I mean, coming around so fast," I said. "Out of nowhere. Uh, I have the homework." I held up the books again.

"Thanks," she said, not reaching for them. "You can come up if you want."

I glanced at her father, but he was already heading back to the kitchen. Jessica went past me quickly, her hair practically brushing my face. She went up the narrow stairs to the second floor. She was still in the same clothes she'd worn to school, still in those thick tights. At the top of the stairs, she took a left.

There was nothing I could do. I had to follow her. It smelled a little like a doctor's office as I hit the landing. The smell was antiseptic. But there was something else, too. Something sweeter. I stepped into her room.

I was surprised to see how girly the room was. The walls were painted a sort of medium blue color. The bed was all puffy, and there were several big pillows at the top. On the floor were a bunch of slippers and a stuffed green frog. A poster of a band was tacked on the wall. All of the guys were striking different poses to make themselves look tough.

The bed was pushed up against the far wall, and the end was right under a window that was open wide. There were a desk and chair against the inside wall and a bookshelf next to it.

The afternoon sunlight was blocked by trees in the yards around the condos, so the air coming into the window was cool.

Jessica sat heavily on the bed. Her hands were folded in her lap as if she were waiting for something. Having been brought all the way to her room, I felt I had to stay for a couple of minutes at least. I slipped into the chair, put the math books on her desk, and dropped my backpack to the floor.

I wondered if she would say anything about leaving school early. Then I thought that maybe I should, but I didn't know what. I opened the cover of the top book and waved it back and forth. "The homework isn't too hard," I said finally. "You could do it easy. There's a quiz on Tuesday on this stuff. Hey, it's a long weekend, remember . . . and a test a week from Monday."

When she didn't say anything right away, I said, "So anyway . . ."

"The elections are that Monday, too," she said. "The seventeenth."

I nodded. "Right. The elections. Yeah."

"Courtney will probably win."

I looked up from the books which I had more or less been staring at. "Really? You think so?"

She shrugged. "Everybody likes her. She'd be good. I hope she wins."

"Me, too." I glanced at her face briefly. A glint of salve or some kind of cream was on her cheeks and neck. That's what the smell was. Medicine. She probably got it in New Haven. I couldn't imagine a fire that would do this to someone.

"You have a nice room," I said, looking around. It sounded lame when the words came out.

Jessica looked at me under the thick folds of skin around her eyes. "I don't know how long we'll be here, but my bedroom is the first thing they do when we move to a new place. My parents, I mean. They brought all my stuff when we came from Boston. I spend most of my time in here. When I'm not at school or at the hospital. It's okay."

She was saying a lot for someone who didn't talk in class.

"My room is small," I said. "This is nice."

"I usually get to be alone here." She kept going.

"Except when my parents come in and yell. They get mad all the time."

"They yell? Your dad seems okay."

"They get mad about me." She moved back on the bed.

Sure, I thought. Because of her sister, right? Because she died? Was it true what people said? Is that why Jessica cut herself out of the picture? Because of what happened?

"They shouldn't bother you," I said.

"Yeah, well, they're parents. What else are they going to do?"

I didn't know what to say to that, so it got quiet for a minute. It still seemed too early to leave.

"I don't know," I said. "Mine are okay most of the time. They wanted me to run for class president. Like that would work. My dad thought of a dumb slogan. My mom bought stencils for the poster and everything. I just sort of shoved the poster into my locker —"

"I hate my mother," she said suddenly.

I shivered. "What?"

"I hate her." She said this without emotion, still looking at me.

"Because she's mean to you? Always getting on your case?"

"She doesn't get on me. I just hate her."

Okay, this was weird. My chest was feeling all buzzy

and electric; my ears rang with a high noise. I fumbled around with the math books. Could I just leave now?

"My mom's okay," I said, trying to change the subject. "My dad, too, pretty much. He thought of this slogan for my poster. A vote for Tom is a vote for *Tom*orrow. Get it? They're okay, I guess."

She shrugged. "Good for you."

Yikes. I felt as if I was going to explode or something. A breeze came in the window and not wanting to, I shivered again. "Do you want me to close the window?"

"No. I like the air coming in."

I nodded like I understood. It was because of the fire, right? You felt trapped. You couldn't breathe, right? I mean, I guess, right? What was keeping me here? Was it okay to leave yet?

"Sometimes I just lie on my bed really still," she said, glancing out the window. "I have to stay really still sometimes when I go to the hospital —" She stopped. "Do you read comic books or something?"

I turned to her. "What?"

She motioned to my backpack. The top edge of Jeff's comics were sticking out from between my books. The red and yellow and orange title was partly visible.

The Human . . .

I quickly pushed them down. "A little. Not much."

"It's not like I care," she said. "I read them in the hospital sometimes, when there's nothing else. It's so dumb.

They think all kids read comics, so they have them in the ward. Somebody donates them."

I imagined rows and rows of beds with burned kids screaming and moaning in them.

I tried to be light. "Really? Which ones do you like?"

She shrugged, and I felt like an idiot. Of course she doesn't have a favorite, you dork! She doesn't read comic books. Why would she read comic books? This is insane. I'm going.

"What do *you* like?" she asked. "*Superman?*"

"*Superman!* No way," I said, almost instinctively. I shook my head, wanting to end it all right there. But the way she just kept looking at me, I began to think that maybe she was talking because she didn't get a chance to talk much. After all, when was the last time any kids came to visit her? And she just said her parents yelled a lot. She stayed in her room all the time. Plus, her sister, who she probably at least hung out with, was gone and everything.

"Well," I said, "I mean, Superman has super everything. X-ray vision and super strength, and he can fly. It's sort of too much power, if you know what I mean. He can do pretty much anything he wants. It's not real."

"It's a comic book."

I snorted a laugh. "I know, but still. You shouldn't have all those huge powers. It makes everything too easy. Who's going to stand in your way? You'd win every time. Small ones are better."

Was I going *there*? Why was I going there?

"What do you mean?" she asked. "Small ones?"

I fidgeted. "Small powers. Never mind. It's too stupid to talk about."

She said nothing, but sat there waiting for me to go on. Just like Mrs. Tracy had waited for me to say I would bring the homework.

"Small powers?" she said.

I laughed. It was a nervous-sounding laugh; I knew that. But I tried to make it sound natural. "It's dumb. But it's just that, you know, you have the ability to fly and X-ray vision and superstrength and stuff. But sometimes I think it's probably better to have a really dumb power."

"A dumb power," she repeated.

"Something really dorky and useless, like, I don't know, having one indestructible finger or something. I think that would be really cool."

Oh, man, was I really saying this?

She looked down. "A finger? Why just a finger?"

I sat forward in the chair. "Because otherwise it's like asking for too much. If you want to be immortal or to fly or to control people's brains or something, it's like you think you deserve this huge ability. But if you're regular in every other way, but just have one indestructible finger, who would ever say no to that?"

"So you don't ask for too much."

"That's right. It's just something small and cheap,

what no one else would ever think of. It's so much better that way."

"Something nobody else wants," she said.

"Right," I said. I realized then that I had never said any of this out loud before. I wasn't sure why I was telling her then, except that maybe I thought it didn't matter. Who else would she ever tell? Even if she made fun of me, it would be okay because it would end here. "But maybe the best part," I said, "is thinking how you could turn that really small dumb power into something completely awesome."

She scratched her arm as she thought. "What could you do with an indestructible finger?"

I shrugged wildly. "I don't know. Maybe you could stop an attacking animal or a runaway airplane just by sticking your finger out. Or scratch into the earth with it and find something you need, or poke right through the door of your enemy's hiding place. Stuff like that. The more you think about a little power, the more big things you come up with. Pretty soon, you find you could do anything."

"What would they call you?"

I laughed. "I don't know. Superfinger?"

"Power Pinkie?"

I laughed again. "Or what if your power was that you could whistle really loudly? You aren't that strong and you can't climb buildings, but you go in there and tell them they better stop or you'll whistle very loud. It's so dumb your enemy just laughs at you. While he gets ready to use his vapor vision on you, you whistle so loud his eardrums hurt, and he gets an instant headache. Then you move in on him because his hands are up here —" I put my hands over my ears and screwed up my face as if I were in pain.

She nodded like she understood. "Uh-huh."

I laughed again and found myself leaping to another idea. "Or what if you could skip really, really fast?"

"What would you do? Just skip around?"

"I don't know, yeah. People would be stunned by how quickly you could get to them. *Whooosh!* You're across the room! Then you skip around them and make them dizzy just watching you. Having dumb powers is like having a secret identity because no one knows you have this power until you use it. Mostly you're fairly useless; nobody thinks you can do anything at all. Until you really need to do something; then it comes out. I mean, the more you think about it, the more you realize what cool things you can do with the lamest powers. You can do a lot."

I stopped to breathe and was suddenly totally exhausted hearing myself talk. I thought now that she was bored and might just be pretending to listen.

Then she said, "If I lay really still on my bed, and if there's a breeze, it feels like I could glide right out over the yard. Not fly really, but just sort of swim in the air. Slow."

"Glide? Yeah. That's good."

"The wind goes through the leaves in the trees and I feel like I could move out into it. I figure if I go out far enough I'm not here anymore."

I looked at her for a second, then away. "Uh-huh."

We sat not talking for a few minutes. She was still sitting on the bed. I was in the chair, looking around her room.

Then I remembered the reason I was there and told her exactly what the math assignments were by reading out Mrs. Tracy's note, and showed her the pages in the book, although of course she could find them. But I found myself flipping to the pages in the book and even coming over and putting the book open on the bed next to her so that she wouldn't have to move.

I didn't even want to, but while I was standing over her I sniffed in with a little quiet sniff. I don't know why.

She glanced up at me suddenly.

Oh, no. Did she hear me? I stepped back —

"Superheroes are supposed to do good things for people, aren't they?" she said.

"What?" I asked.

"They're supposed to help them, right?"

"Help them . . . sure . . ."

"Well, it might be hard to actually help people with just a loud whistle or skipping around in a circle."

I frowned. "I guess. That's always harder to do."

In my daydreams I always ended up saving Courtney from some nutty enemy so she could fall in love with me or whatever. But helping?

My mother was all about helping, too. Why did everybody have to wreck things by talking about helping people? Having small powers now seemed totally stupid and pointless.

Time to go.

"I better leave. I have a church thing."

I went to the door and out to the landing outside her room. When I turned I found her looking straight at me. She had followed me there and was standing close.

"Uh, sorry about your sister," I said.

She looked right at me, not blinking. "Thanks for holding my hand for the prayer thing," she said.

"Oh, yeah, sure. Sorry about all that."

"No one really touches me anymore."

What was I supposed to say to that? "Uh-huh."

"Do you want to touch my face?" she asked.

I felt my own face go red. My legs became icy. I think I teetered on the landing.

"Uh . . ." I raised my hand a little, but Jessica pulled back from me right into her room and closed the door. I heard a brief slapping sound, like a book being closed. Then I heard what must have been the squeak of bed-springs as she lay down.

Chapter 14

When I got to the bottom of the stairs, my legs felt like water. I turned and found Jessica's father standing in the living room.

"Sit down for a minute," he said.

Oh, man, no. Please, no. I have to leave. But I couldn't think of any way to just get out of there. He moved over to a big chair, so I sat down.

The corners of the room were full of moving boxes. The few pieces of furniture — a couch, three chairs, a low table — seemed placed any old way around the room as if Jessica and her family had moved in only minutes before.

Nothing matched, for one thing. The chairs were all different fabrics and clashing colors, too big for the room, and they were old.

Rich had said that the Feeneys were hiding out from the police, and probably their furniture came from the dump, which is where all criminals get their furniture. You could prove it by calling the dump to ask if anything was missing.

Remembering that, I nearly laughed, except that the air in the room seemed so heavy it probably would have sucked away any sound. Then Mr. Feeney started asking questions. General stuff, like about St. Catherine's and my family and where I lived and stuff. Nothing very deep.

There was a picture frame on the coffee table that was mostly turned away from me. I leaned in to try to see what it was and was shocked to find that it was a larger copy of the little one that had fallen out of Jessica's pencil case: her sister and her father at the beach club. Except that this one wasn't cut off on the side. I was suddenly all confused.

I had expected to see Jessica in the picture. Instead, there was an older brown-haired woman standing there. She was smiling, too.

A terrible idea had begun to grow in me, just like it had when I first saw the picture in school.

"I saw this," I said, moving the frame around so that we could both see it, "but not all of it."

Looking at the woman, I guessed it was Jessica's mother. But if Jessica didn't cut herself out of the photograph, where was she? I glanced around the room, but I didn't see any other pictures. Well, of course not, stupid.

Why would anyone want to torture her by having a picture of the way she used to look and never will again?

"That was a few weeks before the accident," he said.

The accident. It was an accident. I nodded. "Sorry."

"Jessica likes it," her father went on. "Well, I don't know if she *likes* it, but she wants us to keep it around where we can all see it. I don't think it helps anybody. Not me, for sure. And not Mrs. Feeney. Jessica wants to . . . I don't know. . . ." He sighed.

"I'm sorry," I said again. I knew I had to say something, but I didn't know what. I looked closely at the girl. She really was beautiful and fun-looking, with that little smile on her lips.

"It must have been really terrible," I said. "I remember when my grandfather died. I was little, but I knew that everybody was upset because it was sort of sudden. I'm sorry, it must have been bad when she died."

"When she died," Mr. Feeney repeated softly. His eyebrows wrinkled. "I thought you said it was your grandfather that died?"

I looked at him. I started to feel sick again. "No, no. It *was* my grandfather. I meant when *she* died." I motioned to the picture. My hand was trembling. "Her. Jessica's sister?"

"Jessica's sister," Mr. Feeney said, leaning over the table almost as if he was going to jump at me. I was shaking. "Jessica's sister? Who do you think you're looking at? She doesn't have a sister. Where did you get the idea that she has a sister?"

I kept staring at the picture, trying to get it. Words formed in my head, but they got all garbled on my tongue. "But she had it in school . . . and somebody asked her if it was her but she said . . ."

"No, no, no, no," he moaned, jerking back into the chair. "That is Jessica. That is Jessica."

My blood froze. Oh, god, no. It *is* her. The smile on that girl. I just stared at the picture and kept staring because I couldn't get it, I couldn't get it, and I didn't want to see his face again. My stomach was twisting inside me. This girl is Jessica? Where is her face? Where did it go? Oh, no, no, no.

"I'm sorry," Mr. Feeney said, slumping again into his chair and letting out a huge breath. "Did Jessica play a trick on you?"

My chest heaved suddenly, and my throat felt thick. I shook my head. That wasn't it. That's not what happened.

"She's done it before, I think. She's done lots of strange things. I'm sorry she did that. Jessica has her ways of dealing with what happened I guess."

We were silent for a while. A part of me couldn't believe that I was talking to her father; the burned girl's father.

"I'm sorry she did that," he said again.

"So . . . how did it happen?" I said finally, surprised at the way the question just came out.

He made a short gesture with his hand, as if it was so long ago that there was no point in telling it all again. He seemed to go inside himself, but then he started rambling around and around for a while as if he didn't want to go over the old story and didn't want to say all the words again, but couldn't stop himself. From what he did say, I sort of pieced together an answer.

Sometime when Jessica was in the sixth grade, she and her mother had gone to a place called World of Dance or Dance World to pick up tickets for a recital Jessica was in. She loved dancing as much as she loved tennis and biking.

While Jessica was waiting out front in the car — which Mr. Feeney said was still running — some old man had a kind of attack while driving down the street in his truck. He was going too fast and smashed into the back of the car Jessica was in, ramming it really hard into the car parked in front of it.

Gasoline burst from the gas tank and went everywhere inside the car. Everything caught fire and so did Jessica. Because of the flames and the heat and the truck jammed against it, it was a while before anyone could get her out. Her mother came rushing out of the dance place, but she couldn't get anywhere near the car. No one could.

By the time the fire rescue trucks arrived, most of Jessica's body was burned.

I couldn't stop myself from crying while Mr. Feeney was saying all this, amazed at what he was telling me. Finally, he stopped, shrugged his shoulders again, and settled back into the chair.

Wiping my face and trying to keep my voice low so that she wouldn't hear what we were saying, I asked him, "Will it get any better?"

The expression on his face showed how many times people had asked him that. He smiled stiffly and said, "A little. Over time. Not right away."

But how long would it be? Will I see her as she looked before? Could the doctors make her look like the picture again? Were they even trying for that? Could they do it? Could they find her face under all that?

"We try not to think about how long it might be," he said. "It's hard. Every time a doctor says something your mind goes on, you know? You want it so bad. It'll be . . . it's a long road. She'll never look the way — like that again. But that's only part of it. Her lungs were badly damaged. The circulation in her legs. But I couldn't imagine going on without her around. We love Jessica. More now than ever before. We're glad she's alive. That's pretty much it."

And that was it.

Mr. Feeney rose from the chair as if he were balancing a big sack of something heavy on his shoulders. He wobbled for a couple of seconds then made his way back to the kitchen. He started cleaning again.

To my horror, I heard someone rushing back up from the bottom of the stairs. Jessica had been listening. Oh my God.

I left, going past her father and out to the side step just as a minivan was pulling into the driveway. A woman got out, holding a bag of groceries. She had brown hair that was pushed back behind her ears. This was the mother Jessica hated.

I stopped in front of the garage door next to the back step. I wondered what she would sound like. She was there, after all, two years ago, when the thing happened to Jessica. She'd left the car running. Did that make a difference?

"Hi," I said. "I'm Tom. . . ."

But she must not have seen or heard me, because she didn't say anything. She went around the back of the car, opened the rear door, and pulled out another bag of groceries. She was thin and about as tall as my mom, but seemed small somehow and shorter because she was bent over the bags she was balancing. She went past quickly and in the side door, which Mr. Feeney opened for her, but I didn't hear them say anything to each other.

On the way home, I felt as if I had been beaten over

and over with a baseball bat. I just couldn't imagine being burned like that, trapped in a burning car. And she was alive and going on. She was going to school! It was too much to understand, too much to get. I started crying again, and when I got inside I rushed to the upstairs bathroom, where I got sick.

Chapter 15

"My uncle's coming in four days," Jeff said on the bus first thing Tuesday morning. "He called last night."

The long weekend had gone by so slowly. Jeff was out of the picture, spending the three days with his father in the city. On Sunday, my mom and dad and I drove up forever on a bunch of long, windy roads to a little town named Kent, where we bought two small pumpkins and three big ones for Halloween ("Too many," my mom said, "but that's okay!") and I drank too much cider.

Most of Monday I was in and out of the bathroom, but I felt better by the time the school bus came the next morning.

Through it all, through the drive and the cider and the bathroom, I had spent pretty much every minute thinking about the picture and Jessica's face and what her father told me and how small her mother seemed all pulled inside herself and how Jessica said she hated her.

Hated her, I guessed, because she'd left the car running and didn't save her. Or couldn't save her. I don't know.

The whole thing about the dead sister, the questions from the Friday before — all of it seemed pointless now. It was so completely meaningless. I wasn't even going to try to put into words what I now knew was true about her. The other kids didn't matter now with their stupid stories. It wasn't anyone's business anyway.

Watch. I won't say a word. They'll all know I went to her house, but I won't say a word.

"Cobra time."

Or should I tell them? And what should I tell them, exactly?

"Tom," said Jeff from the seat next to me. The bus was pulling into the school parking lot already.

I turned. "What?"

"Cobra, Saturday."

I almost didn't hear him. That hour at Jessica's house. Listening to her. To her father. Something's different now. I'm different now. I know more than anybody about how it happened. About the sister thing. There was no sister. I know about what she went through and still has to go through. I shivered as we got off the bus and stepped down to the sidewalk in front of the school. She had heard her father and me talking about her. She knew that I knew what nobody else knew. Was that bad? I wasn't even sure.

All I kept seeing in my mind was her car in front of the dance place. First I imagined that it was a minivan. When I remembered that they actually had a minivan, I decided it had to be a regular car, a Toyota or a Taurus. First new . . . then old . . . forest green . . . then maroon . . . then black. The more I tried to think of something else, the more I saw the car all covered in flames and the more I saw Jessica's face. Each time a wave of sickness came over me.

But Jeff kept saying stuff. At least five more times before first period — on the playground, in the lavatory, in the hall. Saturday, he said, was going to be the day. Our day.

"My uncle's coming. Noon. Noon is gonna be Cobra time. You and me, Cobraman. Rich wanted to come over, but I told him no. Even Eric asked, but I don't want him peeing in the car."

All morning he went at it, not saying a word about my lie of having to help my mom at church, but whispering, even in religion class, a little chant: "Cobra . . . Cobra. . . ." He tapped his pencil to get my attention then showed me where he'd drawn a picture of the car in the margin of his notebook. "Cobra . . ."

Each time Jeff told me, I just said, "Yeah, great." On Wednesday he did the same thing, and I kept on trying not to show any emotion about it. I couldn't believe, didn't want to believe, it was really going to happen, because I didn't want to get suckered into waiting for the car to come. I wasn't sure that it even meant anything to me anymore.

Jessica wasn't in school. More tests and treatments, I guessed. It was amazing how school sank right into being like before she had ever come. I didn't hear anybody talking about all the crazy sister ideas of last week. School was just school again.

By Thursday morning, when Jeff was still at it with his "Cobra, Cobraman, oh, yeah," a thought was beginning to grow inside me, as if it was swimming up from somewhere deep down.

And the thought was that maybe I deserved this.

After all, I had done the tough thing, hadn't I? I'd done more than anyone else had, right? I'd actually gone to her house. I knew all about Jessica. I'd been in her room. Talked to her. I even talked to her father. Who else had done that? I heard the truth about the accident. I knew what happened. I had cried, too. It had been so strange going to Jessica's house, but I did it. No one else did it. I did.

"We'll drive by Courtney's house at noon," Jeff said, grinning as if it were his idea. "I told her you wanted to."

"What?" I finally said, turning to him. "You *told* her?"

"She'll be waiting," Jeff said with a nod. Then he

headed into first period, leaving me stuffing books into my locker.

Jessica still wasn't there. Maybe she wasn't going to be in all day again.

So, okay, I thought. Okay. It's cool that Jeff doesn't care that I skipped going to his house and went to see her instead. So maybe we will drive by Courtney's house. She'll think I'm cool. Maybe she'll even go for a ride with us. It's possible. There are only two seats, but we can squeeze. That would be cool. And when I nominate her for the election next Monday she'll thank me. We're back to that, now. The Courtney thing.

It was me and Courtney, after all. How long had it been since I even thought of that? With all the craziness going on, I'd almost forgotten to think about it. All the adventures. The earthquakes. Volcanoes. Marauders. Our pockets full of money and stuff. Tearing off in the car. That's what everything was about. That was the main thing. Tom and Courtney.

Not Tom and Jessica. What *was* that?

A warm feeling came over me, like something familiar was happening. I thought of roaring away in the Cobra, from Courtney's house. Of rolling uphill to a lost temple of terror. Of leaping from a crashing plane, holding hands.

No Jessica. Courtney.

When I slammed my locker door, the sound echoed

down the hall, and I thought about all of it. I crossed the hall to the water fountain and took a long drink, letting my mouth fill with cold water. I closed my eyes.

Yes. The car and Courtney and me. Saturday bright and early. No. Noon. Noon was Cobra time, right? I smiled. I breathed in slowly, swallowing the water in small gulps. Things were simpler already.

"Thank you, Tom."

I almost spit the water out on my shoes.

Thank you?

I lifted my head from the fountain and turned to face the light shining in the hall from the doors at the end.

Only, it wasn't Courtney. It was Jessica's bulky shape silhouetted against the light coming from behind her. Suddenly, I don't know, my heart sank. It was her again. Farther back beyond the doors stood her father, looking so tiny as he leaned in to watch her go.

"Thank you," she said again.

I stood all the way up. "Okay. But for what?"

"For the homework. I never thanked you for bringing it over. I ended up taking the math quiz today because I've been out all week."

I wiped my lips on my shirt cuff. She seemed tired. "Oh. Sure. No problem."

"I've had stuff to do every day at the hospital. I've been pretty out of it." She paused. "You look happy."

"What?"

"You're smiling really big."

"Oh, yeah, well . . ."

I was happy. I felt good. I had brought her the homework. I did that. Now it was my turn. The Cobra was coming. I would take my ride in it. That was the thing I had been waiting for. Nothing could mess that up now. Jeff had promised me.

I decided I was going to be big about it.

"You know what?" I said, trying hard to be casual. "Are you going to be around tomorrow at about noon?"

"I think I'll be in French class. Where will you be?"

I thought for a second. "Not tomorrow. Saturday. Will you be around. I mean at your house?"

"Unless I'm at the beach," she said.

"Huh?"

"It's a joke."

What? What's with all the jokes?

"Actually," she went on, "I was going to ask if you wanted to go to New Haven with me and my dad on Saturday. I have to see a doctor, but you could . . . I don't know, hang out on the green or something with him. For a little bit. Then we can have lunch. There's a place we go to where they know us —"

"Saturday?" I said, confused to hear her talk about the day of the Cobra.

"Around ten. Just for a couple of hours and then back." She made a little shrug with her shoulders that reminded me of the girl in the photograph. Of her, the way she used to be.

"I can't," I said. "I can't. I'll be . . . I'm waiting to ride in a Cobra. I was going to say that if you were around, you could check it out. It's so cool."

"A Cobra?" She just stood there.

I hadn't planned for this. A Cobra? Who doesn't know what a Cobra is?

"It's a sports car," I said. "There aren't a lot of them. It's really fast. Jeff's uncle has one, and he's going to drive by and take me for a ride. If you're back from your doctor you can see us cruising around. I'll ask him to drive by your house."

She looked at me. What was in her eyes just then? Suddenly, I'd felt just as stupid as when I told her about the superhero thing. What was I doing? And what was she, bored? Disappointed? Never mind; I knew what it was. She didn't like Jeff. That was it. She hated him because he wouldn't hold her hand. And, of course, she hated cars.

I don't even know why, but I kept going.

"There really aren't a lot of Cobras around," I said for the second time, "but it's definitely the coolest thing on the road."

More looking. Those heavy eyelids. What is she waiting for? I've done the tough thing already. Wasn't I even talking with her now? Do I have to go to the hospital with her? Do I have to keep doing more? Do I have to feel bad about riding in a car and thinking about Courtney?

"Have fun," she said, turning to go into the classroom.

Does everything have to be about being burned?

Chapter 16

She was wrong about being there on Friday. She was out again, as usual. So that was all we said to each other the whole week. I thought about calling her Friday night to remind her that I'd be driving by, which I was still going to try and do, but what else could I say that I hadn't already said? Besides, she had made me feel so stupid about still hanging with Jeff and thinking that a car was really cool. And Jeff was my friend, wasn't he? At least I had history with Jeff, all those afternoons at his house. I decided to just forget about the whole thing and not bother her.

Saturday morning dawned bright and warm.

I called Jeff early to nail down the exact time he'd be there, but his phone was busy and, besides, he'd told me like a thousand times that they'd drive by at noon.

Cobra time. Yeah.

It was actually good his phone was busy. Preparations were being made. Wheels were in motion. Cobra wheels, flashing in the sunlight. Ha. I pulled out my car magazines and looked at the pictures, reading my favorite parts again. I needed to be able to talk to his uncle when I met him.

At 11:30 there was nothing else to do, so I camped on my bed and peered out my little window to watch cars passing the house. The air coming in was warmer than it had been the day before. Summer was hanging on for another day. It was so much warmer than it was supposed to be. Perfect weather for a convertible. I wondered if Courtney was waiting for us. Jeff had told her we were coming. Then I thought of Jessica maybe looking out her window, too. No, it was probably too soon. She was still in New Haven. She wouldn't be home yet.

I closed my eyes and tried to imagine gliding out over the yard the way she had talked about, but I kept peeking whenever I heard a car drive by. It wasn't working. Flying wasn't my thing anyway. It was too big. Never mind. It's Cobra Day.

Back to Courtney. What was she doing? She lived in a big green house not too far away. I smiled when I thought of flicking my indestructible finger at marauders and roaring off with her in my fast red car.

Noon came and went. Jeff said they'd be here at noon. It was after twelve o'clock. Then 12:15 came, then

12:25, 12:40 . . . I called him again. There was no answer this time.

Finally. They're on their way.

One o'clock. Had I gotten the time wrong? The day? I mentally checked to see if it was really Saturday, running through the last few days — doofus, of course it was Saturday! Still, I checked the other three clocks around the house. It was just after 1:10 on all of them.

Positioning myself on my bed again, I waited some more. At twenty after, I made another call. No answer again. Something began to start inside me. Was I surprised that Jeff was so late? I wanted to be, but I wasn't really surprised. This was Jeff, after all. It wasn't practical to think he could do stuff by a clock or be on time for things. So, okay. Jeff was just late as usual. And uncles, of course. You can't count on them being on time, either.

Car after car passed by. Almost two o'clock. I called Jeff's house again. No answer. So, okay, I could have gone with Jessica if I'd wanted to, which I didn't.

The something inside me was oozing into my stomach now. What was it? Not anger, not yet. Almost, but not yet. It was something else.

Was Jeff mad at me? Was he getting me back for the whole Jessica-homework-lying thing by being late? No. That meant that he had to plot it all out. He had to promise that we'd go for a ride in my favorite car and then not do it. He had to think up a big plan about the car and his uncle and give me times and things. You had to put a lot of thought into getting back at somebody that way.

I looked out the window. No cars passed by for a few minutes.

Jeff didn't care about that kind of stuff. He didn't even think that way. It was like his shirt, how he dribbled red juice all over it and didn't care that he did it or who saw it. Or the Batmobile he torched. Or the things he said about Jessica, or even about Rich and Eric. Or how he treated his mother. He probably said things about me, too. Jeff didn't care when he did that stuff. He didn't care now that he was late. He didn't know what other people wanted, and he didn't really care. That was it. He didn't care.

Three cars in a row, none of them a red Cobra.

Jeff hated it when his parents broke up two years ago. Now, his father didn't want him to visit so much, and his mother was always working. They didn't care, so he didn't care.

He lied a lot, too, didn't he? Was he lying about the blood on his mother's uniform? I don't know. I'd never seen it. I'd never really seen the Cobra either. Maybe there was no Cobra. Maybe there was no uncle!

I lay on my bed still looking out the window but letting my gaze go unfocused. What if Jeff had lied to me about the car? Would that even surprise me? I had a sudden thick feeling in my throat. My chest felt hollow and sick at the thought, but I had to tell myself that the answer was no. I wouldn't be surprised.

Jeff was a liar. A liar who didn't care.

Two thirty came. Quarter to three.

Now I got mad. It came boiling up inside me and I started fuming around. Shaking now, I went to the phone in the kitchen and dialed Jeff's number again.

"Hicks house," Jeff chirped into the phone.

"So you're home? Where's the car?" I blurted out.

"What? Tom? Hey, what's up?"

"The car," I repeated, swallowing back a catch in my throat. "Where's the car? The Cobra. You said you'd drive by at twelve o'clock. Your uncle was coming over, remember? Are you coming over now? It's three. Where are you?"

There was a muffled scratching on the other end of the phone. "Obviously, I'm here. Talking to you on the phone —"

"Did your uncle come over today?"

"What? Yeah, he was here."

"Well, did he have the stupid car?"

"Oh, it's stupid now? What's your problem?"

"Did he have it with him?"

"No. He didn't."

"So you lied," I shot into the phone. "You said he could — he'd drive by and we'd go for a ride. Well, where are you —"

"Lied?" he snapped. "What do you mean? That I didn't come over on purpose or something?"

"Why didn't you call me?"

"What are you, my girlfriend?"

There was a pause. I could hear him starting to breathe hard. "So he didn't bring the car today," he said. "So what. My mother needed stuff moved. He brought his other car. I told you she needed to move stuff. She says we might have to move to a different house because my dad's not paying —"

"So why didn't you call? You were talking about it all week. You told me like a hundred times that you'd come by with the stupid Cobra. You didn't say anything about moving stuff. You said we could go see Jessica and pick her up —"

"Jessica?" snapped Jeff.

I froze. "I mean Courtney."

"What does Jessica have to do with this?"

I felt my throat closing up again. It was getting out of control now. I should just hang up.

"You told that girl about the car, didn't you? And you're calling me a liar?"

I could hear voices raised in the background.

"So what?" I said. "Yeah, I told her. I wanted her to see the car. I love Cobras. I was going to wave or something."

This is pathetic. It's stupid. Stupid. It's so out of control. Hang up. I hate it.

"Wave to her?" Jeff said, his voice rising. "The car isn't here today. This is so weird. Why do you even talk to her?"

I didn't have an answer. I tried to swallow. The voices were yelling now and Jeff was moving with the phone.

"I'll tell you something," he said. "I'm glad when she's not in school. It's so gross sitting behind her. My uncle wouldn't let her anywhere near his car, even if he had brought it." He started to laugh now.

"Shut up," I said.

There was the sound of a door slamming.

"Yeah, shut up," he said. "I knew there was something off about you. The Human Dork meets the Human Torch. You went over to her house and now you're all about her. Freaking firegirl! Why would I take you to her house? I just want to run away, she's so freaking ugly! There aren't supposed to be people like that. Why does everything have to be so ugly — ugly, ugly, ugly —"

I cursed at Jeff and slammed down the phone.

I ran up to my room and stayed there for the rest of the day. My mother called me down for supper, but I pretended at first to have a headache. She came in later, but I was in bed with my eyes closed and pretended to be asleep.

Both of my parents checked on me. They came quietly to the door two or three times. Once my father said, "Tom?" But I didn't say anything. They left me alone after that.

Waking up on Sunday, I was all achy and exhausted. As soon as I sat up, I remembered that I'd had a dream during the night. I felt nervous, and my stomach got all twisted in knots when I remembered it.

In the dream, Jessica was in a black car. The car had fins all over it but was crunched up into a mess and was burning. You could see her pounding like crazy to get out . . . pounding on the windows and then falling down inside the car, out of sight. Everyone was rushing around, but the fire was too huge for people to get close to the car. I tried to get close, too, but kept being pushed back. Her mother was trying to get to the car, too. Then somehow Jessica was out of the car screaming. I turned and pushed my way through the crowd and ran away from her. I ran and ran and ran. Then I woke up.

Chapter 17

Monday was class election day. Jeff wasn't at the bus, and he wasn't in his seat in class. Maybe he wouldn't be in at all. I wished he wouldn't be. But Jessica was. She was sitting quietly in the seat next to mine when I came in. The whole day before, I was worried she might call to ask where I'd been on Saturday after lunch, because she didn't see me or any awesome sports car. But she didn't call. Maybe she was at her doctor's all day anyway. It didn't matter.

I was too mad to talk to anybody on Sunday. I barely said anything to my parents, even though they asked me a few times what was going on. But now, in the minutes before class got started, I couldn't stand it. I turned to her.

"The whole car thing didn't happen," I said. "Sorry."

"Neither did New Haven," she said. "I was at home."

How stupid. "Sorry." That was all we said.

Mrs. Tracy came in, and we stood for morning prayers. When they ended, Jeff walked through the door and slid into his seat. His expression seemed hard and empty. His jaw was grinding as he stared off at the windows, and his legs were twitching. He seemed like some kind of animal ready to bolt up and out of there at any second.

"All right, then. Today is the day we've been waiting for," Mrs. Tracy said, starting the big business of the morning. "The election we've been preparing for."

Something cold dripped through me. It was like a trickle of ice seeping down my throat and into my chest. I glanced over at Courtney, who was sitting quietly in her seat. This was it. The moment. I tried to put the whole Jeff and Cobra thing out of my mind. And that stupid dream of Jessica. I didn't even know what that was about. I tried to breathe deeply and slowly. My hands were trembling.

Okay, Courtney. I knew it would be so awesome if I could really do what I had wanted to do for weeks now. Me and Courtney. It was like swords were suddenly flashing around me, explosions were everywhere, there was a boiling river below me, and an avalanche above. I breathed in and tried to stay calm.

The door clicked as Mrs. Tracy closed it. "We've heard some speeches and seen some posters."

"Darlene's is the best," said Samantha Embriano.

"Thanks," said Darlene, a bright red dot on her chin.

"And now the time has come for our primary," Mrs. Tracy said. "When you nominate a candidate, it should be someone who has made a poster that made you think, given a good speech, or somehow proven that he or she would be a good president. Once we zero in on our candidates, we will vote by secret ballot. I'd ask you to keep in mind that this is not a popularity contest. It shouldn't be. The winner will be our first elected class president, an office which carries a lot of responsibility. Lots of fun, I think. But whoever wins this morning will come to meetings, form groups, and help organize events, so there is a lot to do."

She looked around and everyone quieted down. "Are we all ready? Then let's start. Who wants to be the first to nominate someone?"

Everyone waited. It was perfect.

My hand shot up, and Jeff shouted, "Courtney."

I gasped. "What —"

But Jeff didn't look at me. He just bobbed his head around to the back corner of the room. Courtney's face turned red at hearing her name, but she was smiling. Lifting her own hand, she said, "I'd like to nominate Darlene Roberts."

I couldn't believe it. Jeff had wrecked everything. Courtney was mine. He knew it was my idea to nominate her. I noticed Rich looking at me. He knew it was my idea, too. He was there when I told Jeff about it. It wasn't

Jeff not caring this time, though. He did it on purpose. He had planned it.

Now it was too late to do anything.

I heard Kayla naming Samantha Embriano next. Dave fidgeted in his seat and seemed to be waiting for someone to say his name. He caught Kayla's eye; she shrugged and nominated him, too. Samantha frowned.

Joey nominated himself then retracted it, naming Eric LoBianco instead and laughing through it all.

Mrs. Tracy wrote the names on the board. "Anyone else?" she asked. "No more? So, we have Courtney, Darlene, Samantha Embriano, Dave, Eric . . ."

Jessica's hand went up.

"Yes, Jessica? Would you like to name someone?"

In her small, breathy way she said, "Tom."

It was as if I'd suddenly been zapped with a thousand volts of electricity. A hundred thousand. Every part of me felt a jolt of hot energy. What did she say my name for? I'm no candidate. I didn't even show anyone my poster. I didn't even want to be president — not that anyone would vote for me. Then I thought Mrs. Tracy might object because I didn't campaign, but she didn't.

"Jessica named Tom," she said in the same plain way she said everything else. Then she chalked my name on the board beneath the others.

It was so strange, so embarrassing to hear my name connected with Jessica's. With all those eyes turning to me, Jeff even turning, I felt my face go so red. I didn't want this. I didn't deserve it. The images in my dream rolled back again.

I felt finally as if I had lied a really horrible lie (worse than any of Jeff's), and now that Jessica had named me, everybody knew the lie. I was suddenly ashamed and angry with myself. I wanted to run. My stomach churned. I felt cold.

"Good. Any other names?" Mrs. Tracy asked.

Then a strange thing happened. If I felt nervous and ashamed, the other part was that I felt I had to do something. My name was right up there on the board with everybody else's. The teacher had written it the same way she had written the others. The same way she had written Courtney's.

And now that Courtney was already nominated — stolen from me by Jeff — it seemed there was only one thing I could do. A thing no one else would do. And I had to do it. The only way to get Jessica into the class, really into the class, was for one of us to get her in.

I mean, why not? I don't know if anybody would vote for her, but Jessica was smart and nice and she'd been to lots of schools, so she knew how things worked. And she even made that joke about the beach. Maybe the only way she could really come into the class was if she got involved. We would all get over the problems about her being burned and different and just get down to business. Maybe this was even better than nominating Courtney. I would do it. I would.

Mrs. Tracy looked around again. "Is there no one else? Are we all done nominating?"

I swallowed hard. "Jessica —"

"Well, all right, then," she said, turning to the board to scratch numbers next to the names. "We have Courtney, Darlene, Samantha, Dave, Eric, and Tom."

And Jessica.

Sweat poured down my chest and onto my stomach. The sides of my shirt were soaked. My waist was soaked. I glanced around the class. They were all looking at the board. No one was looking at me. Even Jessica's head was down.

I turned to Mrs. Tracy again. She has to write Jessica's name. Add the name. Do it now.

Mrs. Tracy set down the chalk and dusted her hands. "Six altogether. Three girls. Three boys. Good."

She hadn't heard me.

Did I even say it out loud? I didn't!

Mrs. Tracy stepped to her desk and picked up the voting slips, and suddenly it was too late to do anything. I couldn't say Jessica's name now. That would be stupid. My mouth wouldn't even work. I was suddenly a tiny invisible thing with no voice. Too small to do anything. And it was too late.

"We'll now begin our voting," she said.

Confused, hot, my blood racing, I tried to busy myself with the tiny piece of paper and my pen. But there wasn't much you could do to make yourself busy with such small things. I stared at the little yellow slip.

"Please vote by writing the name or the number of your candidate on the paper, and then fold it over," the teacher said. "When you have voted, raise your hand and Ryan will collect the votes in a box. Ryan will not look at the votes."

A few minutes later it was all over.

Ryan collected the votes and Kayla tallied them. Mrs. Tracy laughed and said that Kayla's skill in math would probably not be strained by counting only twenty-one slips of paper. Then the teacher recounted them herself and gave them back to Kayla to announce.

"Courtney won seven votes," she said. There were cheers and applause. "Darlene four, and Samantha Embriano three."

Eric and Dave had two each. Joey did end up writing his own name on his vote, but then crossed it out, disqualifying himself altogether.

"There's one vote for Tom Bender and one that was blank," Kayla finished.

Jessica turned to me after the tally was read. "Sorry," she said, as if she were apologizing to me that I got only one vote. "You should have voted for yourself. A vote for Tom . . ."

She didn't say the rest of my stupid slogan. Right. Vote for myself. So I wouldn't be dead last, the bottom of the list, the complete loser.

But I was the loser. I didn't do anything. How could I vote for myself? I didn't vote for Courtney or even Jessica, who I wanted to nominate. It occurred to me that even if I couldn't manage to nominate Jessica, I could at least have voted for her. I could at least have done a write-in vote. But no. I couldn't even manage to do that.

All I did was prove that I was just like everybody else when it came to her. I was like everyone who ignored her or was afraid of her or hated her or wished she didn't exist. Like all those people running around her burning car. They didn't get her out. They watched and ran around all stupid, but they didn't get her out. And now she was like this forever. Even here and now, she was still in that car. Like every single one of those people, I did nothing. I ran and ran and ran.

"Jessica," I began to say, "I . . ."

She just did a sort of tight, painful thing with her lips and kept her head down.

After I got home that afternoon, I called her house, but after three rings I hung up. I could have held on longer or tried again. I knew that. But I didn't right away, and the day sort of flew by with stuff to do. Yard work. Emptying the dishwasher and reloading it. Ironing my uniform shirts. Cleaning my sneakers. It was just stupid little stuff around the house that seemed to take me forever. I ended up not trying again, and then it was suppertime.

After we ate, the phone rang. "It's Jeff," my mother said. My father looked at me when I didn't take the phone. I didn't move, then told my mother to say I was busy and couldn't answer.

A little later, the phone rang again.

"Tom, phone," said my father.

"I'm not here. I'm at the mall with Mom."

"It's a girl."

I felt tired all of a sudden. I just wanted to sleep. "Hello?"

"Hi. It's Jessica. Can you come over?"

I breathed out. It suddenly seemed the hardest thing in the world to go over there. I didn't want to see her. Please. Her father with the "Sit down, Tom." What more was there? I felt so tired.

My mother was looking at me from the counter. "I guess," I said. "Sure. Okay."

Chapter 18

The sun was just under the horizon when I made my way across the yard and down the sidewalk to her street. I remember thinking that night was coming sooner these days, even though it was still warm. Good. I was already so tired by everything that had happened, I just wanted the day to end.

Why did she even ask me over? What was she expecting? What did we have to talk about? And why was I just going over as if I had nothing to do? Okay, sure, I'll drop everything and come. I was so tired. I stopped.

This is stupid. Why should I go there? So I didn't nominate her. So what? Did I have to? Was I supposed to —

A rumbling sound came from somewhere behind me.

I turned, and even before I realized it, the Cobra was there, coming fast around the corner, tightly hugging the curb. I froze as it roared up the street toward me, its headlights blazing.

So here it was, after all. The awesome Cobra. As red as blood and fantastic. I couldn't believe it. I just stared.

"Hey! Woo-hoo!" came a shout from the passenger seat. Jeff was sitting next to a man with thinning, peppered hair who wore a blue sweatshirt with ragged, cut-off sleeves.

The uncle. So he did exist.

The engine gave out a sudden gunned roar as he rolled the fat car up really fast, then braked sharply, three or four feet away from me. Even stopped, the car looked as if it were moving. It was clear it was just pausing for a couple of minutes before roaring away. The engine sputtered and popped like gunshots. The street vibrated under me, and the thundering went up my legs.

I still couldn't believe it.

"Woo-hoo!" Jeff hooted again, arching up. "Get in!" He stood in the seat, swinging the little scoop neck door open for me. The car was so red. The finish was deep, liquid and hot, just like at the car show that time.

"Tom, this thing is so fast," he said. "You won't believe it. We've been everywhere. Come on, we'll go get ice cream or something. My uncle's paying."

The guy at the wheel checked his watch, then he gave a nod as the car inched nearer to where I was standing. Heat poured up from it.

"Come on, Cobraman," said Jeff, grinning. "This is for you, you know. I made him come up here from the city. On a Monday night. I told him you really, really love this car and you gotta ride in it now!"

I looked at him, then at the uncle. The half-bored grin on the man's face was what I imagined Jeff's might look like someday.

"Come on," said Jeff, his eyes still fixed on me. "We'll drive past Courtney's house. I already called her to tell her we'd stop by. There's enough room for all of us, if you guys squeeze in with me."

I looked in at the seats. Could I fit in there? With her? Man.

I looked across the street at Jessica's house. Lights were on downstairs.

"So let's do it already." Uncle Chuck looked at his watch again, and the car rolled forward. "I gotta get back."

I didn't move.

"What?" said Jeff. "Are you coming?" He glanced across the street now, too. He must have known it was her house. "Come on, Cobraman, let's fly. Or are you going to see her? I can't believe it. Will you let it go? The Cobra. Are you the Cobraman or not?"

"Don't —" I said, holding my eyes on Jeff.

"Don't what?" he asked.

"Don't call me that."

"This is crazy!" he said. "Why are you just standing there? Do you love her or something? Look. I got him to come here for you. Don't be a dork."

I felt as if I were a wire filled with electricity, burning up. My chest felt ready to burst. My jaw was tight. My feet tingled. I was so stiff that I felt I could lift right off the ground like a statue or something. I just stood there forever between taking a step and not taking it. Then all of a sudden I sort of jerked in front of the car. It rolled toward me and I felt its heat pouring on my legs.

"Don't be a dork. Get in."

"Jeff," I said, "why don't you just —" My breath caught suddenly in my throat and I had no voice. I finished what I was saying by flicking my finger toward the end of the street.

"Freaking firegirl!" Jeff said. Then he came out with a curse, said it again, and slumped back into the seat, yelling, "Let's get out of here!"

"Hey, I don't give a —" the uncle said, slamming his foot down and ripping off down the street, swaying wide around the far corner and away.

I looked there for a while, then turned toward the black square of screen on the side door of Jessica's house.

Every part of me was shaking as I went up to it.

Chapter 19

I was in her house again.

Her mother was sitting at the kitchen table when I knocked, but it was her father who came from another room and let me in. "She's upstairs," he said. Her mother looked at me, and smiled slightly when I went by, but she didn't get up or say anything. Her hands were folded around a cup. There were papers spread over the table in front of her.

I went upstairs to Jessica's room. The last of the day's light was fading now across her wall. She was sitting on her bed, as she had been the first time I went to see her.

"Hey," I said. I wanted to sit at the desk again, but her chair was piled with clothes. I sat at the other end of the bed. Right off, I wanted to say I was sorry for the way the election thing had been all goofed up, but that there was always next time. And even now she could help Courtney on some project or something. Even I could help. That would be the way to do it.

"Today was so dumb," I started. "But I was thinking —"

"I'm leaving," she said.

I looked at her. "What?"

"I'm leaving on Wednesday. I won't be back in school."

I felt as if somebody had just punched me in the chest. "What?"

"It's not working out," she said. "We thought it would work out here. That's why we rented this place. It was supposed to be until Christmas, at least. But the doctor doesn't like how it's going. . . . There's a thing with my circulation, and he wants me to go back up to Boston again."

I wasn't getting it. "It's only been like three weeks. You should be here more. You have to be here more."

Words were getting jumbled in my head and on my tongue. I was sweating again, and I didn't even have my uniform on. I tried to look into her eyes. I knew they were so green, but the light was nearly gone. "I mean, you can't —"

"You can get back to normal in school now," she said.

That was just too much. I felt myself begin to lose it. My eyes stung. "Jessica . . . don't . . ."

"Don't what?"

"Don't hate me. . . ."

"I don't. What for?"

It was coming out now, and I was mad. "For today! For the whole stupid thing! I should have talked to you more. Said more stuff to you. But I didn't. I don't know why, but I didn't. I'm just like every other idiot."

"No you're not."

"I didn't do anything!"

She breathed out. Then she said quietly, "It doesn't matter. I really have other stuff. Important stuff. About getting better. Or not getting better. Every time I go in the hospital, I find out all over again about what really matters. This doesn't."

I was shaking, imagining the hospital, then the car, and Jessica on fire inside it. Tears started boiling up out of me. "But people are actually scared of you," I said. "Of the way you look. They don't want you around. You have to hate them —"

I noticed she was trembling now, her hands shaking in her lap. "Sure I hate them. You don't even know. But there are always some people who won't be that afraid."

"I'm afraid!" I said, surprising myself because I thought it was the worst thing I could say, but it was true. "The way you look . . . it scares me. I'm too scared to be close or nice to you. I don't say anything. I don't talk to my parents about you. I never talk to you where anybody can see me —"

Jessica laughed abruptly. "Who cares who sees you talk to me? Besides, you said my name; that was something."

I turned to her. It was getting so dark in the room I almost couldn't see her face anymore. "You heard me?"

The night sounds were starting outside the window.

"You really have to speak louder," she said.

"I'm such a jerk!" I said, laughing and crying at the same time. "No one else heard it —"

"It's okay. Besides, I'd probably only get one vote, so I'd never win. Then you'd feel a lot worse."

"Yeah," I snorted. "You'd be tied with me as the loser."

"A vote for Tom," she said. Even though I couldn't see, I could tell there was a smile on her face when she said that. You can tell if someone is smiling when they speak.

For the next few minutes we didn't say anything. I wiped my face and rubbed my hands on my pants. The room was almost totally dark now.

As the minutes went by and we didn't speak, the silence went around and around and dropped down over us like the night dropped into the room. It was strange, but it was okay. It was good. We were quiet, both of us, in her dark room. I practically couldn't see her anymore. She was just the shape of a person. But I felt that of all the places I could be — at supper, in my room, watching TV with my parents, in Jeff's car, anywhere — I was in the one place I should be, doing what I should be doing.

The room darkened finally and completely. I still knew the rest of the world was outside the window, but it was okay without us. Everything was just waiting for us to finish what we were doing.

"It's dumb to ask for a lot now," she said after a while. "It took me a long time to figure it out, but when I throw up or pass out or hurt all over or get some new test results, it seems stupid to want to be pretty or to have friends or to fit in or to be in high school. I just feel amazed each time I wake up after a treatment and still know who I am. My mother . . . my mother was the first one with me when I woke up after the accident. She gave me this —"

She moved in the dark and I just made out that she took the stuffed green frog from her pillow and held it up.

"You said you hated her."

She shook her head. "Sometimes." Then she said in a whisper, "I was so afraid. . . . Tom . . . do you know what I did when I woke up the first time? After the accident?"

"What?"

"I asked her if I was still alive or if I had died." She turned to me. I was crying again. "Isn't that the dumbest thing? And she didn't say anything; all she did was cry and cry. I guess she didn't know what to say. I didn't know then what I was like. Isn't that the dumbest thing? To ask if I was alive?"

I wiped my face and remembered what everyone had said. That they couldn't believe she was alive. "It's not dumb. I'm glad you're alive."

"Me, too. It's different now, but I'm glad."

"It's a good thing to be," I said. "You could do a lot with just being alive."

She breathed out a quiet almost-laugh. "Because you shouldn't ask for too much, right? You told me that."

Boxes were being shoved downstairs, chairs thumped on the floor. Silverware and dishes were clanking together.

"You have to pack?"

I saw her nod. "Yeah. The moving people are coming in the morning."

My chest was pounding.

"Bye, Tom."

She was just a shape in the dark, and I leaned over and sobbed like a baby and hugged her. I haven't hugged my mother in probably two years. But while I held Jessica it seemed the only thing to be doing. It was long. When I moved away, my cheek brushed against hers. It was wet, too.

"Bye."

Outside, the street was empty and the night was clear, quiet, and blue. When I got to my room, I lay in the dark for a while, just being quiet as the cool air streamed over my bed. I imagined her face as it was now. It faded into the one in the picture, then moved away and came back different still.

Chapter 20

The following morning, Mrs. Tracy announced to the class that Jessica was moving to Boston for more treatment. She would not be back in class.

Some kids mumbled a couple of words. A few even said it was too bad, we were just getting to know her. But there wasn't much real talk about it. Now that Jessica was gone, we all felt like a heavy weight had been lifted from our shoulders. Everyone had wanted that to happen since the first day we saw her. Finally, it was okay to be goofy and loud and dumb and regular again.

As Mrs. Tracy started into science, I glanced up from my desk. Courtney looked as if she were going to jump up and storm right over to me, but she didn't.

Jeff didn't say much all day, and that was fine with me. After school, I went straight home. From the little window in my room I could just see the back end of the moving truck parked in front of her house. I actually started over there. I wanted to see her again, I wanted to talk to her again. But halfway to the corner, I stopped. Beyond the front of the truck, in the driveway, I saw her mother holding a cardboard carton under one arm and pulling at the minivan door with the other. She tried once, twice, then finally got the door to slide open. Jessica appeared at the kitchen door, nudging it open with her arm. She dragged a thick duffel bag out onto the step. I started walking over again, but when Jessica lifted the bag across the walk to the car, I stopped again.

Mrs. Feeney turned around and then moved back. I guess she was surprised to see Jessica so close beside her.

Jessica looked at her mother and then pulled something green from the opening of the duffel bag. It was the stuffed frog she'd shown me the night before. She plopped the frog on her mother's arm suddenly. Then she hopped it jerkily across her mother's shoulder to her cheek and leaned it in as if it gave her a kiss. After a moment, she pulled it back, nuzzled it for a second, and then put it into the bag.

All this was done without either of them saying anything.

I watched as her mother helped Jessica stow the bag and then went back into the house with her, slipping her arm around Jessica's waist. That was all there was to see.

I turned and went back home. The rest of the

afternoon, I just lay on my bed. Movers went in and out of the place, carrying boxes and furniture, less and less each time. I spent Jessica's last day there staring out the window until it got dark.

The next morning I looked out, but the truck was gone, and of course the minivan was gone, too.

The air was cool. Fall had finally moved in. It took me almost the whole day before I realized I wasn't sweating like I had nearly every day since school began.

In fifth period, I caught Courtney looking at me again. She did nothing then, but at the end of the day, as the last buses were called, she surprised me at my locker.

"You were nice to her," she said, coming out of nowhere. "To Jessica."

Her voice was soft and nervous. Looking into her eyes that close, I was surprised to see after all this time that they were gray.

"I didn't do anything much," I said.

"You did. You must have. She nominated you to be class president. Because you were nice."

That last word stung. I started shaking my head. I had so wanted to get all the feelings out of me for good. When Jessica left, I wanted all my mixed-up thoughts about her to leave, too. But it was like they wouldn't go. Now as I stood there, the hallway thinning out, they came flooding out of me.

"I don't know why she did that. I tried to nominate her, but I didn't get to. I wanted to do so much, but I was so stupid and so sc — scared . . . and now she's gone —"

My nose burned suddenly and my eyes filled up. "I'm sorry, this is so dumb." I started to turn, but Courtney reached out and touched me on the arm. It was a light touch. I saw that her eyes were wet, too.

"I think you probably made her feel better than anyone else did," she said. "You went to her house. You took her her homework and everything."

I shook my head again. "Mrs. Tracy told me to."

"But you went. No one else did." She stopped for a few seconds. "Anyway, she had at least one person here who she liked. She liked you."

I wiped my eyes and swallowed. "Maybe."

"I'm pretty sure."

That was all.

I didn't go to Jeff's house in the afternoons much after that, even though a couple of weeks after Jessica left, he began inviting me again. He didn't move or go to public school after all, but it was too much of the same stuff all the time, and I just didn't want to hear it. Hanging with him and talking and laughing at the stuff he did didn't seem right anymore.

My mother asked me why I didn't go to his house like I used to, and I said that the seventh grade had more homework.

"I have to stay in the good reading level," I told her.

My excuses to Jeff were pretty lame, too: I had to clean my room, move some plants, rake my grandparents' yard . . . After a while, he stopped asking and did more things with Rich instead.

I thought it would never be like the way Jeff and I had done stuff, but with his empty house after school every day, at least he had somebody to hang around with, and Rich was okay.

Jeff moved back into the seat next to me, and he and I still talked in school. Sometimes he was pretty funny. But it wasn't the same between us after Jessica.

At first, I wondered how long she would even remember being at St. Catherine's. I mean, what was the big deal with us? The way she went from city to city and school to school, how could she remember one class over another? All the faces staring at her like ours did. Everyone so afraid of her. We must all blend together and get mixed up after a while. She had more important things to deal with than to remember all the dumb people around her. She had to live. Her days were filled with stuff so bad I could barely imagine it.

But I did try to imagine it.

I found myself zoning out in class, wondering what was happening to her. If she was in some hospital. If she was in another school and was it high school this time, where she should have been. Where in the classroom they put her desk. Did they make up stories about how she got burned? Did she still have that picture with her? Was she looking any different? Would she live as long as me?

On the outside it doesn't look like very much happened. A burned girl was in my class for a while. Once I brought her some homework. In class she said my name. Then she was gone. That's pretty much all that had happened.

I wish I could say I was a better person because of Jessica, but I'm not sure. Every now and then I wonder what she would think of the things I do or don't do. Would she get mad at me like an older sister would? Would she smile like when she said "A vote for Tom" that time in her room?

Once, on a cool night, I imagined we were talking in her dark room again. Everything quieted down and it was just us. I told her I talk to Courtney more now, but that she's not in my adventures so much anymore. I don't know who it is because her face keeps changing. Then, even though I knew I was talking for both of us, Jessica said I should take all those snake pits and detachable ears and invisible elbows and find a way to do something really good with them.

Maybe I will. Maybe tomorrow I'll get out there.

One thing I know. If I ever saw her again, I think I'd

start saying all kinds of stuff and probably wouldn't be able to stop. And I'd want her to talk, too. A lot. I'd want us both to talk to each other deep into the night and not stop. Mostly, I'd want to tell her thank you. And I'd try to say it loud enough for everyone to hear.

Acknowledgments

I owe a debt to everyone who read this small story as it took shape, especially my agent, George Nicholson, who championed it through thick and thin and for longer than I did myself; Craig Walker, among the very first to help a little idea blossom into something bigger; Patricia Reilly Giff, my teacher and friend, whose comments were, as always, completely inspired and completely correct; Paul Rodeen, who saw potential and followed through on it; Alvina Ling, my delightful and sensitive editor at the very beginning of our relationship; and finally my wife, Dolores, to whom I am indebted in ways far deeper than words can express.

Tony Abbott is the author of over sixty books for young readers, including the bestselling series The Secrets of Droon and the novel *Kringle*. He currently lives in Connecticut with his wife and two daughters. *Firegirl* is his first book with Little, Brown.